# THE LAND GRABBERS

## D. B. NEWTON

SAGEBRUSH
Large Print Westerns

First published in the United States by Popular Library

First Isis Edition
published 2018
by arrangement with
Golden West Literary Agency

A catalogue record for this book is available
from the British Library.

ISBN 978–1–78541–551–7 (pb)

Published by
F. A. Thorpe (Publishing)
Anstey, Leicestershire

Set by Words & Graphics Ltd.
Anstey, Leicestershire
Printed and bound in Great Britain by
T. J. International Ltd., Padstow, Cornwall

This book is printed on acid-free paper

Johnny Logan, a Cheyenne raised by a white adoptive father, figures he's found a good berth as a rider on the Bar J spread — until the rustling begins. Out patrolling the ranch one day, he sees a terrified Cheyenne riding hell for leather, heading for the sanctuary of the nearby reservation. Then the man's pursuers — including Dallas Howbert, owner of the neighboring ranch — appear, claiming they were chasing a beef-stealer. Having lost their original quarry, they drag Logan before the sheriff, accusing him of conspiring in the escape of a thief. It's only the intervention of his boss that sees him released. But Logan is convinced that the Cheyenne are being unjustly blamed for cattle poaching. For there are many people with their eyes on the reservation's land, who will stop at nothing to see its inhabitants driven out . . .

# CHAPTER
## ONE

A brief spatter of sound, somewhere in the rounded grassy hills to the north of him, was unmistakably gunfire. Johnny Logan heard it and instantly halted the bay he was riding, reining the horse around and lifting his head sharply to listen. For a long count of ten there was nothing; then, just when he was about to turn away, two more shots followed each other closely, and after that a third. Moments later he was able to make out the first noise of horses running hard.

Someone was in trouble.

The mouth of a draw choked with aspen and pine growth emptied directly above him. The hoof sound came down from there, on a constant wind that combed sun-browned grass and breathed steadily against his narrowed eyes. Tricks of acoustics caused the sound to swell and fade again, as the animals were ridden hard over outcrops, or through timber that sopped it up and muffled it.

But the riders were definitely making in his direction and coming fast. Though there was no more firing, caution made him reach down and push the tail of his denim jacket out of the way, clearing his holstered gun. He was debating whether he should find some cover to pull back into, when the first of the riders suddenly plummeted out of the timber.

Johnny Logan closed his hand on the butt of the six-gun, but he didn't immediately draw it.

The rider came pelting toward him, down out of the draw, letting his spotted animal pick its own tricky, flat-out course. His head was turned, unshorn black hair whipping about his face as he watched for pursuit. He rode without a saddle, an antiquated-looking Sharps rifle held straight out from his body, while with the other hand he managed the rope hackamore that served him for a bridle. An unbuttoned shirt flapped behind him and showed a thick torso that was dark-skinned, slabbily muscled.

He was an Indian on a stunted Indian pony, and he seemed to be running for his life.

The fugitive squared about now and for the first time saw Johnny Logan waiting, almost in his path. The sight struck him. The pony lost stride for an instant under the jerk of the rider's hand. The Sharps swung around as though he meant to try an offhand shot with it — surely the powerful jolt of the weapon would be enough to unbalance him and knock him off his horse. But then Johnny Logan solemnly raised his empty right hand palm forward, in the universal sign of peace.

Black eyes in a broad, dark-skinned face peered at him. Until that moment the fugitive had no doubt seen him simply as another faceless enemy like his pursuers, this one bent on blocking the road. Now the Indian seemed to recognize Johnny, or at least to realize that the eyes he looked into were as dark, the face as bronzed, the hair under the brim of the other's hat just as coarse and night-black as his own.

For all that Johnny Logan might wear the gear of a cowpuncher and sit a white man's stock saddle with a white man's sixshooter in the holster at his waist, he was as much a Cheyenne Indian as the fugitive himself. The latter's pony held for a brief moment, on short rein, moving about restlessly. The Sharps was lowered until it rested against the thigh that clamped the animal's heaving, sweated barrel. And Johnny raised his voice across the intervening distance: "Friend, is somebody after you?"

Another, nearer burst of hoofsound, scattering out of the higher timber, gave him his answer. It jerked the fugitive's head sharply around while the long hair, thick as a horse's mane, whipped about his naked chest. Then the man settled himself, and a kick of his moccasined heel drove the paint once more into its reckless gallop. He gave Johnny Logan a single desperate look as he pounded by; after that he was gone, swallowed up in brushy folds of land, the drum of unshod hoofs quickly fading.

Johnny Logan swore, and it was a white man's oath. Letting the Indian go, he turned his stare back up the throat of the draw. As he deliberated, the answer to one nagging question suddenly came to him: He was sure he had seen that broad-cheeked face among a group of braves he'd met once on the nearby Cheyenne reservation — men he remembered from Lame Elk's village. The fugitive's name was Badger. It had stuck in Johnny's mind, because he thought at the time that the man looked remarkably like the animal he was named for.

It was pure, blind terror he'd read in Badger's dark face just now, and that wasn't a thing a man could ignore. Almost without thinking, Johnny Logan swung his bridle and spurred his animal up into the draw, tracing backward the flight of the fugitive.

The going was steep, rubble-strewn and treacherous; it was a wonder Badger hadn't broken both his own neck and his pony's. Johnny Logan picked his way carefully, and presently the scrub timber closed around him and the branches shifted overhead, with a flickering of sunlight and shadow. He got through a tumble of boulders; he heard the riders coming.

They broke into view directly ahead — four of them, appearing so abruptly that he had time to do no more than pull broadside to them, hiding the right hand he cautiously dropped to the butt of the gun in his holster.

If anything, the riders were even more startled than he. They hadn't expected to see anyone blocking their way, and they hauled rein some dozen feet from him. The leader was a rancher named Dallas Howbert, and Johnny Logan recognized two of the others as riders on Howbert's payroll.

They all had guns in their holsters, and he saw a couple of rifles thrust into saddle scabbards.

Howbert was staring angrily at him. As the horses stirred uneasily, having been checkreined so suddenly, the rancher demanded, "What are you doing here, Logan?"

"This is Bar J. I work here."

Howbert was a sullen man, with thinning hair and a perpetually sour look about him. His face colored now, and he snapped, "Don't bicker with me! We mean to go through here. Do you have it in your mind to stop us?"

"I might," Johnny said crisply. He was trying to watch all four at once, still in the dark as to what was going on but well aware that these men had terrified Badger into panicky flight.

The one who appeared to be a new hand on the payroll was peering at him closely, and now the fellow said, "Who *is* this man, Mr. Howbert? I'm damned if he don't look Indian, himself — even if he don't talk like it. Or dress like it, either."

"He's Cheyenne," the rancher answered shortly. "I understand some Indian lover took him in as a kid, gave him his name and brung him up white — and right now Arne Jenson has him on the payroll. I'm damned if I know why!" And then, to Johnny: "Logan, I think you know what we're after. Are you going to get out of our way? Or make us run over you?"

Dark face expressionless, and making no move at all, Johnny said, "Is four to one your idea of fair odds, Howbert?"

"The hell with fairness!" The rancher made a downward slicing motion with the edge of a palm. "I've finally got a chance at one of those reservation beef-stealers, and nothing's stopping me — least of all, another damned Indian!"

But one of his men, known to Johnny Logan only as Chris, told Howbert drily, "Looks to me you're already stopped. We ain't that far from the reservation. He'll be

5

just about across the line by now. We're never gonna catch up with him."

The warning hit home. Howbert plainly saw the truth of it and scowled. He swore fiercely, and Johnny's tension eased to know that Badger was safe.

Then the six-shooter lifted from the rancher's holster, and its black muzzle settled squarely on Johnny. "At least, we got this one!" Howbert grunted. For an instant the breath squeezed tight in Johnny's throat. The man was angry enough to shoot him out-of-hand.

Instead Howbert said gruffly, "Chris, take his gun." Not questioning the order, the puncher kneed his mount forward and rode him around to the downward side of Johnny's bay, being careful not to get between him and the leveled weapon. Caught by surprise, Johnny Logan offered no resistance as Chris lifted his revolver from the holster.

Someone suggested, "We going after the first one?"

Dallas Howbert shook his head. "Not much use, as Chris says. He's safe by now — thanks to his friend, here!"

All eyes rested on Johnny Logan with such stern hostility that he felt his mouth go dry. The only suggestion of what he had stumbled into had been Howbert's angry remark about beef-stealers from the reservation; and that was ominous enough, taken against the background of recent event and rumor that loomed like storm clouds above the horizon.

"Bring him along," Dallas Howbert said gruffly and lifted the reins.

There was no further explanation, and with Chris at his flank to urge him Johnny didn't argue. The other two hands fell silently in behind, and Howbert led the way. They rode northward, back up the timbered draw.

Wire fences were taking over much of Montana, but there were places where boundaries were still poorly marked — as here between Bar J and its smaller neighbor, and between them both and the sprawling Reservation of the Northern Cheyenne. But Johnny had spent enough time riding line and turning back strays, that he knew most of the landmarks; he could tell they had crossed onto Howbert's grass by the time they dropped into a swale, bringing into sight the motionless red of cowhide and brighter red of blood.

The butchered animal was a young one, from last spring's calf drop. Johnny Logan saw Howbert's Rafter H brand. The animal's throat had been cut and bled out generously. He saw evidence that the knifehandler had made some first moves toward cutting up the carcass but must have been interrupted.

Johnny didn't ask for details. He thought he'd be told what they meant him to know.

At a word from his boss, Chris got down and, with some reluctance, broke out his slicker and managed to wrap the bloody carcass in it. He slung the bundle up behind his saddle and lashed it there, cursing the horse, which bridled at the smell and tried to make trouble. While Chris quieted the horse, Howbert told his other punchers, "You two get on with your work. We can handle this." They turned and rode off without a word, though they gave the prisoner some cold parting looks.

Howbert looked to Chris mounted again now, who nodded that he was ready. "Let's go, then," the rancher said shortly.

Temper was beginning to have its way with Johnny Logan. "Do you mind letting me know where you think you're taking me?"

Howbert's lips thinned down to a slash. "Why, where did you think? To the sheriff, of course. You're going to jail!"

"*Jail?*" the prisoner echoed. "I haven't broken any law!"

The sudden ferocity that heated the cowman's eyes stopped him. Suddenly Howbert's gun was in his hand and the barrel lifted, like a club. "I'll argue with no damn' Indian!" he cried in a voice that shook slightly. "Now, you shut up! Or I'll shut you up with this gun-barrel across your skull, and you can ride in face down over the saddle!"

Johnny Logan's jaw clamped hard. He had never thought of Dallas Howbert as a personal enemy, but now he saw he was up against anger that had gone beyond rational dispute. The reason wasn't far to seek. These were bad times, with passions and strong feelings running high — though until today, Johnny realized, he had never really understood just how far out of control things might have gone. In moments like this a man was wise to keep his mouth shut, ride with the situation and hope for the right decision.

So he merely took up the reins and fell in between his captors. They rode in a heavy silence, unbroken

8

except for the noise of their gear, the creak of leather and the swish of prairie grass about their horses' legs.

Monroe was a cattle town — hub and center of a wide stretch of range country, as well as the county seat. As such it might have given promise of a very fair-sized community, but the truth would have been a disappointment: a criss-cross of dirt streets that were either baked into hard ruts or turned into instant quagmires by the line storms that regularly walked these Montana prairies; a scattering of business houses a surprising number of which were saloons, surrounded by a fringe of mean frame houses behind wooden fences; and a few trees to give what shade there was.

But it was neither worse nor better than the run of such towns — a place to do business, a place to meet and exchange range news, a place for relaxation in the infrequent breaks from the monotony of hard and risky labor. Johnny Logan saw nothing to criticize.

This being Saturday, the ranch crews would soon be in for their weekly celebration. Even this early, though, the town seemed already filled with a transient population Johnny Logan looked around in some astonishment, even though he'd heard enough about the situation here to have had a certain amount of warning. Not many of these strangers had the look of working ranch hands. He saw sunburnt men in farmers' overalls and heavy shoes, others with the business suits and soft hands of townsmen, still more who looked like the sorriest kind of rootless drifters. A good many, apparently, had brought families with them — on a flat at the edge of town, in a circle of canvas-topped wagons and tents, pitched helter-skelter amid scattered trash, men and women were working over cook fires with kids and dogs running underfoot.

Main Street echoed to the tread of traffic along the wooden sidewalks, and in and out of the winnowing doors of the town's saloons. Everywhere, it seemed, men stood arguing. At one intersection a crowd had gathered to hear the harangue of someone standing on a soapbox and reading aloud from the newspaper he brandished. At the office of the Monroe *Weekly Advocate*, other men were clustered around a bulletin board posted outside the door.

Riding between Howbert and the puncher called Chris, Johnny Logan heard the latter's angry comment: "Lousy boomers! Bunch of landhungry scum, every last one of 'em — hoping to grab whatever they can lay hands on!"

Howbert looked over at him. "That's all right, Chris. You don't have to like them. In their own way, they're on our side. They help make a noise. Sooner or later Congress has got to listen and do something about that problem on the reservation. So I guess we can put up with the nuisance."

"Tell that to the boys," Chris retorted, scowling at the noise pouring out of a saloon they were passing, "when they come in tonight and fight their way through this mob — to find the bars have already been drunk dry!"

10

There was a studied insult in the way they talked past Johnny Logan, and through him, as though he wasn't there. He clamped his jaw and looked straight ahead, showing nothing of his feelings.

They rode past the courthouse, which was a blocky frame building with the county offices on the lower floor and, upstairs, a low-ceilinged courtroom where the circuit judge held his monthly sessions. The sheriff's office and jail were in a smaller separate structure next door. Here the three dismounted and tied their horses to the chew-marked hitching pole, and Chris got the bundle wrapped in his slicker.

"Johnny?"

Johnny Logan turned his head. A young fellow named Bob Early, a puncher like himself for Arne Jenson and his best friend by far among the white men on the Bar J crew, was coming toward them, looking puzzled at the sight of Johnny's present company. "What's going on?"

Johnny Logan would have spoken, but Howbert gave him no opportunity. "Get inside," the cowman grunted and shoved his prisoner in the direction of the sheriff's office. Johnny could do no more than offer his friend a shrug and a shake of the head. Early halted in his tracks, frowning; Johnny Logan was being herded, without ceremony, inside the jail.

Sheriff Zach Gifford, a soft-looking man with tremendous jowls and a wide bald spot that he tried unsuccessfully to hide by combing a few long strands of black hair across it, was dozing in his swivel chair behind a desk. The desk was flat-topped, marred by spur marks and whittlings and cigarette burns and numerous rings made by whiskey glasses; the file cabinet, the deal table in one corner and the three straight chairs lined along the wall, looked equally shabby and long-used.

As the three men entered, the sheriff opened his eyes without moving from his position and scowled at them; he didn't look fully awake. But when Chris dumped his burden on the desk top and started to undo the slicker, the lawman jumped convulsively, catching a glimpse of what it contained. He slammed his chair back from the desk and against the wall behind him, as he exclaimed, "What the hell! Get that damn thing *out* of here!"

"It's evidence," Chris told him.

"Don't make any difference what it is!" The sheriff flapped his hands at it. "I don't want that on my desk!" He was still puffing angrily, as the other shrugged and gathered up the bloody carcass. For want of anything better to do with it, Chris carried it to the door and simply dumped it on the ground just outside.

Gifford looked sternly at the rancher. "Howbert, just what the hell is this about?"

"If you'd only look at that animal," the latter answered, "you'd see it has my brand on it. I brought it to prove my case against this prisoner. I want him charged and jailed."

"He butchered your animal?"

"No," Howbert said, overriding a hot protest from Johnny. "It was one of them reservation Cheyenne. Chris, here, and a couple of the other boys are my

12

witnesses. We heard the critter bawling and got there just as he'd slit its throat and was getting ready to carve it up. He ran for it. We chased him across a corner of Jenson's range and would have caught him before he made it back to the reservation — if this Logan fellow hadn't stepped in, to help him get away."

"Logan," the sheriff repeated the name. He hunched forward across his desk, cold stare focused on the prisoner. "I've heard of you. Cheyenne, yourself — or so I understand. So how come you ain't on the reservation with the rest of your kind, where you belong?"

Standing stiffly before the sheriff, Johnny explained in few words. "I happen to choose otherwise. A rancher named Matt Logan adopted me when I was little, gave me his name and an education. I've lived among whites all my life. Right now I'm on Arne Jenson's payroll."

It was plain that the name of Jenson made its impression, he being one of the two largest stock growers in Sheriff Gifford's county. The lawman pursed his lips and studied the prisoner, head on one side. "I'd heard that you worked for Jenson," he muttered. "Do you help your Indian friends steal beef from *him*, too? Or only from his neighbors?"

That stung Johnny to hot anger. His head came up and he said flatly, "I have never —" But the sheriff wasn't listening. A pudgy finger stabbed at Johnny as the lawman continued, without pause:

"Because, I want to warn you, Logan! If what Howbert tells me is true, I can think of no way you could do more to hurt your people. Do you *want* to see their land taken away from them — see the government pack them up and move every man, woman and child out of Montana, back to the Indian Nations? Do you want the reservation broken up and parceled out to the likes of that boomer riffraff out there in the street?" He inclined his head ponderously toward the doorway. "You know, don't you, that that's the clamor we're hearing more and more, every single day . . . Let me read you what it says in this week's *Advocate.*"

He started to fish for a copy of the newspaper under the junk piled on his desk, but Johnny Logan cut him off sternly. "Sheriff, I know what the paper says. And I know about the boomers flocking into this country, like buzzards — just hoping to be on hand when the Reservation's put up for grabs . . ."

Gifford let the paper go. "Then you surely know how the trouble started! Them people of yours ain't satisfied, letting the government support them and give 'em their grub and their clothing and everything else — clear charity, them not so much as turning a hand! No, that ain't good enough! They got them a taste for white man's beef, and now they won't leave the rancher's herds alone. And how long do they think the people of Montana are going to stand for *that?*"

Johnny Logan drew a slow breath. Hands clenched into fists, he looked the fat man in the eye. "I don't believe this, Sheriff," he answered coldly. "The Cheyenne aren't fools. They know the odds against them. They fought the white man as best they could

**14**

and got licked! They aren't going to start the war again by going after their neighbors' herds!"

A hand fell upon his shoulder; Dallas Howbert hauled the young fellow around to face him. They were nearly of a height, the Cheyenne perhaps an inch the taller. He met the white man's angry stare as the latter demanded, "Are you denying what my boys and I saw today — with our own eyes? Do you deny you deliberately interfered so that thief could get away from us and back across the reservation boundary? *Do you?*"

Johnny hesitated, knowing he had no answer to that — that there was no way he could hope to convince these men of his own complete bewilderment about what had happened. Howbert gave a grunt of triumph at Johnny's silence and turned to the sheriff. "He don't deny it, because he can't! Gifford, I repeat what I said before: I want this man jailed. I want a judge to pass on this business."

The sheriff considered. He pushed back his chair and ponderously got to his feet. To Johnny he said gruffly, "You heard him. The law gives me no jurisdiction over reservation Indians — but since you figure you're too good to live on the reservation, I guess that law don't apply to you." He opened the drawer of the desk and took out a key ring and a large manila envelope, which he tossed in front of the prisoner. "Empty your pockets," he ordered brusquely. "Put your belongings in that."

"This belongs to him," said Chris and laid down the gun he had lifted from Johnny Logan's holster. Johnny

**15**

looked at the gun, and he looked at the trio of unfriendly faces. Slowly, and with reluctant movements, he began to empty his pockets onto the desk.

# CHAPTER
## TWO

Johnny Logan had never before seen the inside of a jail cell — not even overnight, at the tail of an ordinary cowhand's drunken spree. Scrupulously Johnny never touched whiskey: he had heard enough and seen enough of the effects of white man's liquor to know that any Indian was risking disaster to fool with it, and he had never been tempted to test his own resistance. He played safe and left it strictly alone.

So now when the heavy metal door clanged shut behind him, he had to fight a sudden and almost suffocating terror. The cell was cramped and dark, lit only by a small window high in one wall and another in the door. There was a musty stench of stale sweat and old vomit, from the covered bucket standing in one corner. For a moment Johnny thought he would be unable to breathe, but he got past that first panicky revulsion. He took a half dozen paces to the window but could see little from there, except a high board fence, the blank backs of buildings across the alley and a single dusty cottonwood. The strap-iron grille covering the window looked stout enough, and he didn't bother to test it. He stood there awhile, listening to the sounds of the village that came to him and reaching for a few vagrant breaths of fresh air, scented with dust and sun-browned grass and sage.

Presently he turned from the window and groped his way to the bunk, a bare slab of timber chained to the wall, and let himself down there to try to make sense of what had happened to him.

What *had* been going on among the people of the Reservation? He hadn't believed any of the rumors; and working a cowhand's tough schedule, before-dawn to after-dark, didn't give him much time to look into them. Moreover, for most of the past month he had been away, helping with a herd that had to be delivered to a buyer over in the Deadwood area.

But plainly, it had been a bad time to get out of touch. The incident today with Badger, at least, was certainly something more than rumor! Even so, Johnny still couldn't understand why he should be sitting here, stewing with frustration in the county jail — unless it was that Dallas Howbert's anger, for lack of a better target, simply had to be vented on someone . . .

There was no way to judge the passing of time. It seemed hours later that he became aware of angry voices out in the sheriff's office. He listened idly, unable to make out what was being said but not supposing it had anything to do with him. Presently, though, the cell-block door was flung open and footsteps approached, the voices still arguing. A key scraped on metal; the iron door swung wide and he saw his boss, Arne Jenson, and the sheriff looking in at him.

As Johnny got to his feet, Zach Gifford was saying gruffly, "You know I can't leave you alone with him, Jenson."

"You can, and you will!" the rancher retorted. He took a step and recoiled. "And by God, you'll leave this door open!" he told the sheriff. "The stench in there is something foul! Don't you ever clean these cells?"

The lawman scowled and mumbled something, but he knew better than to make an enemy of one of the most important men in the county. He told Jenson, "I'll be out in my office. I hold you responsible for the prisoner not trying anything he shouldn't." He took his gross weight out of the dark corridor, leaving the cell open as well as the office door beyond. To Johnny's relief, better air began to stir as the draft took effect.

"Well!" the cowman said. "Looks like you got yourself into some trouble."

"How did you hear about it?" Johnny wanted to know.

"Bob Early. Minute I hit town, he was waiting to tell me about you getting hauled in." Jenson was a rangy man with a rugged, weather-beaten face. He took a couple of nervous strides and then with arms folded and shoulders braced against one rough wall, he peered at the younger man across the cramped space. "I got the general picture from talking to Gifford — his version of it, at least. Now I want yours."

"Mr. Jenson," the young fellow told him earnestly, "if I've broken a law I don't know what it was!"

"Suppose you start at the beginning, and see what I make of it."

As Johnny talked, the cowman took a pipe from a pocket of his coat. Without lighting it, he sucked thoughtfully at the nib and tapped it against his teeth, his shrewd stare never leaving the other's face. He said finally, "This Indian that got away, he was a friend of yours?"

"Not a friend. I only thought I recognized him."

"A Cheyenne, though?"

"Yes sir."

Jenson rubbed his blunt jaw with the pipe stem while he considered. "In helping him escape from Howbert and his men," he said, "did you pull a gun?"

"I did not! Is that what they say?" Johnny demanded indignantly. "I was damn well tempted, and I guess they knew it — but I didn't use anything but words. Fact of the matter is, my gun was still in the holster when Howbert drew his.

"Look, Mr. Jenson! I had no idea what was going on. All I knew, one of my people had been shot at and was running for his life. There were four of them against him — and anyhow, they had no right bringing a manhunt onto Bar J. I guess I jumped in without even stopping to think!"

"I guess I understand," Arne Jenson said, and he gave a sigh as he pushed away from his lean against the wall. "You and I have discussed this question of poaching. Just because my own beef has been let alone so far is no reason I shouldn't be concerned. But because I trust you, Johnny, and because you were so sure the charges against the Reservation Indians weren't true, maybe I didn't take the thing as serious as

20

I ought to. Now it looks like we may have both been wrong." He stabbed the young man with a probing glance. "You got any suggestions?"

Troubled, Johnny Logan shook his head. "I don't know what to say. I just hope what I did today won't make trouble for *you!*"

"Don't fret about that!" Jenson told him, and dumped his pipe back into its pocket. "I figure you for a good man, or I wouldn't have you on my payroll. And I generally stand behind the ones that are." He touched the young fellow's shoulder. "Hang and rattle! I'll go back and see what I can do with the sheriff."

He turned and strode back into the jail office, leaving both intervening doors wide open; Johnny Logan could see the sheriff seated at his desk. The lawman was sunk deep into the swivel chair and looked rather like a baited bear as he scowled up through his eyebrows at Arne Jenson, when the latter came to a stand in front of the desk. The rancher's angry words rang clearly in the still office.

"Gifford, I think you're letting that badge go to your head!" Jenson pointed a finger at the badge, gleaming dully, pinned to the sheriff's unbuttoned vest. "What one of my riders does while on my range is Bar J business. You got no reason at all to hold Johnny Logan in this stinking jail of yours."

The wattles under the fat man's chin stirred as he shook his head. "Howbert says different. He's brought a charge against Logan — conspiring in the escape of a thief."

"Dallas Howbert don't know straight up!" Jenson retorted. "I can understand how he feels about losing beef, but I won't stand for him evening the score at the expense of one of my crew."

Doggedly Gifford said, "You'll have to tell all this to the judge."

"Who won't be sitting here for nearly another month! How much will bail cost me?"

"You know I got no authority to set bail. Only the court can do that."

Arne Jenson leaned forward and slapped a palm sharply against the top of the littered desk. "I be damned if I hold for one of my men sitting in a jail cell, just when I need him! I want him out of there, Sheriff — in the next five minutes. If you won't take bail, then I'll pledge my given word that he'll show up for trial if there is one. And I think you know my word is good."

Watching the sheriff, Johnny saw him wet his lips. Gifford was stalling. He could not help but know that the man facing him had the reputation of being completely honest. And he carried important weight in this county.

The lawman lifted both hands and let them fall to the arms of his chair in a gesture of resignation. "Hell!" he grunted, and started to push himself ponderously to his feet, apparently intending to release the prisoner. When he saw that the cell door already stood open, his mouth drew down sourly and he slumped back into the chair. He called to Johnny Logan. "All right, you! Come in here . . ."

Johnny walked out into the room. Eyes almost invisible behind their narrowed lids, the sheriff regarded him. He said, "I guess you been listening to all that. I'm turning you out, on your boss's terms. I hope you realize that if you *don't* show up when I want you, it'll be on his head."

Johnny Logan told him flatly, "I ain't doing anything that could make trouble for Mr. Jenson." And the latter added: "If I'm willing to take the risk, Gifford, it should be no concern of yours."

The lawman shrugged meaty shoulders and pulled open a drawer of the desk. He took out the envelope containing the prisoner's things and tossed it in front of Johnny. "Here!" he grunted. "Look and see that it's all there. You'll have to sign a receipt." He added, with a trace of a sneer, "I suppose you *can* write your name?"

Not responding with word or look, Johnny opened the envelope and spilled its contents onto the desk. "What about my gun?" he demanded, indicating the shell belt and holstered weapon that hung on a wall peg behind the desk. Seeing the lawman's scowling hesitation, he suggested, "If it makes him feel better, Mr. Jenson, maybe you better take charge of it for me."

Gifford did look relieved when the cowman went over, took down the gun and wrapped the belt around it. Only then did Johnny Logan pick up a pencil and sign the form the sheriff had laid in front of him.

As he was doing so, the lawman picked something from the jumble of Johnny's possessions — a small bag, fashioned of doeskin, hardened with age and decorated with painted figures. "What the hell's this?" he grunted.

Johnny glanced up quickly and saw what he was holding. "I'll take that, please," he said.

Instead, Gifford turned the bag in his thick fingers, examining the faded markings. "What's it got in it?" he demanded. "Heap big medicine? Mouse bones and owl shit — stuff like that?"

"I've never looked inside. It belonged to my father," Johnny told him curtly and held out a hand. "Do you mind?"

Arne Jenson must have sensed danger signals that the sheriff missed, for he intervened. He explained quickly, "Indians are particular about how a man's personal medicine gets handed around, Gifford." Something in his tone must have got through. The fat man looked at Johnny Logan, whose dark face was all Indian just then — eyes hard, mouth grim, hawkish features savagely angry. The sheriff's own gross cheeks suddenly turned red. Without a word he put the bag in Johnny's waiting palm.

The latter gave him the briefest of nods and slipped the bag into a pocket of his shirt. Then he set about collecting his other belongings — a pocket knife, a few coins and bills, other odds and ends.

Jenson, meanwhile, had a bone to pick. "Since all this uproar started," he told the sheriff, "about the Indians poaching beef from the ranches adjoining the reservation, I'd like to know just what your office has been doing about it."

The swivel chair creaked under the lawman's weight as he turned angrily. "There ain't a hell of a lot I *can* do! The county only gives me one deputy — do you

24

expect us to patrol the whole length of the Cheyenne Reservation? Besides, those Indians are wards of the federal government. County law has no authority to interfere with them, even if we didn't have problems of our own to keep us busy."

As though giving point to his words, a racket of loud voices, and boots trampling the sidewalk, had been rising in the street outside. Gifford swung his head ponderously toward the door. "There's one of my problems!" he grunted, making a face. "Those damn boomers are pouring in here faster every day. The town marshal is eighty years old and less than useless. Shouldn't be the province of the sheriff's office, having to preserve order in the city limits and keep a land-hungry mob from taking the place apart! But who else is to do it?" As the noise continued to grow, Zach Gifford swore and lumbered to his feet.

He moved too slowly. He reached the door and started to close it, but before he had it quite shut somebody outside pushed it open again. The man who entered was cadaverously lean, in wide-brimmed planter's hat, rumpled clothing and a straggling, black string tie; his blue-striped shirt did not look entirely clean. His sidewhiskers were shot with gray, and he had deep-set, beady eyes and prominent teeth that gave him a rabbity look.

Johnny knew him by sight. His name was Nate Rawls, and he owned and edited the local newspaper; some people called him "Judge," though he had never held that office. He had, however, served one term in the state assembly at Helena, which was enough to make him a distinguished man in a place like Monroe.

He acted as though he expected to be treated accordingly. "Sheriff," he began importantly, without preamble, "what's this I hear about someone bringing in a prisoner? One of those thieving red savages —" He broke off as he saw Johnny standing by the desk. He looked at Jenson and then into the empty cell-block. The long lip slid down across his teeth in a scowl. "Is *this* the man? Why isn't he locked up?"

Not answering immediately, the sheriff stepped past him to the street entrance, where his bulky figure almost blocked the view of the clot of men who lingered outside. Angrily, Zach Gifford shouted at them: "Now, you go on — the lot of you! This is no public meeting. Get away before I run you in for unlawful assembly!" And he closed the door on them firmly.

Turning and putting his back against it, he glowered at the newspaperman. "You seem to have influence with those boomers," he said gruffly. "I wish you could do something to keep them in line."

"We're not talking about them!" Nate Rawls snapped. He pointed a bony finger at Johnny Logan. "Is this the prisoner I heard about? He certainly looks Indian to me!"

Arne Jenson answered him in a tone of clear dislike. "This is one of my hands, and he's been released into my custody. Got any questions?"

"I certainly have!" Rawls turned on the sheriff. "Have you any idea — with feelings what they are —

how bad a mistake you're making if you turn this fellow loose? I could have told you, had I been asked . . ."

"But you ain't." Jenson reminded him. "This may come as a shock to you, Rawls, but there are actually some people who don't give a damn for your opinions! Nor are they impressed by that two-bit newspaper of yours, or by the influence you keep bragging about — either at Helena, or in Washington, D.C."

The other heard him out, the eyes smoldering in his gaunt face, cheeks stung slightly with color. "Judge" Rawls seemed able to control his temper, and he said coldly, "You speak plain, at least."

"I certainly hope so!" the cowman told him. "I hope I never gave you cause to misunderstand me. In *my* book, you're nothing but a troublemaker. You been one of the loudest in all the clamor about breaking up the Reservation and packing the Cheyenne off south to resettle in the Indian Nations — something that was tried once before and didn't work, because there wasn't any way to make those people stay in that godforsaken dust bowl!

"That riffraff out there tags you around like you was a tin god of some kind, but *some* of us ain't fooled! We know what you want is their votes, to take you back into politics — maybe, this time, clear to the U.S. Senate."

Sheriff Gifford moved his bulky body between them. "Gentlemen!" he begged. "Please! This ain't getting us anywhere . . ." He seemed uncomfortable at finding himself in the middle of a quarrel. Nervously he hurried to make his point, explaining to "Judge" Rawls,

27

"As for this fellow Logan, there's no evidence he was actually mixed up in any poaching. All he did was get involved in an argument of sorts with Dallas Howbert — and they were on Jenson's own land when it happened. Jenson's promised to see that he appears if and when the circuit judge so orders. Under them conditions, I see no objection to lettin' him go for now."

"I can think of a few," the newspaperman retorted stiffly. "And you needn't think the whole matter won't get an airing in the next issue of the *Advocate.*"

"I was taking that for granted," Arne Jenson told him. And he turned away, shutting off the discussion. He had Johnny Logan's hat, which he had retrieved from the top of a wooden filing cabinet; he handed it to its owner and told him gruffly, "Come along."

Johnny hadn't spoken at all during the controversy that raged around him, and now he hesitated, looking first at Rawls and then at the sheriff. "Where's my horse?" he asked the latter, who answered shortly, "I had it taken to the livery."

Johnny nodded. "Look!" he blurted. "If you'll ask Dallas Howbert what the calf was worth to him, I'll pay for it myself. Will that satisfy him?"

The sheriff returned his look without expression. "I wouldn't pretend to know," he said finally. "I'll ask him. Meanwhile you better see you don't make any more trouble."

Johnny's mouth tightened. "Come on, Johnny," his boss said again. The young fellow shrugged and, pulling on his hat, swung away to the door, where the

**28**

cattleman stood waiting. No one spoke as Jenson lifted the latch and let Johnny Logan precede him out of the jail.

# CHAPTER
# THREE

In the street outside, talk broke off and there was a general lifting and turning of heads. There must have been a couple dozen of the boomers who had followed "Judge" Rawls to the jail and were now split into animated groups waiting for him to emerge. When they saw Johnny Logan and his employer, everyone fell still; Johnny sensed hostility as the eyes of these men settled on him. Plainly, they all knew exactly who he was.

Johnny hesitated an instant, but Arne Jenson's hand was on his shoulder. The rancher said gruffly, "Pay no heed." He turned the younger man along the walk, and was close at his side as they started away from there. A big red-bearded fellow, who might have been some kind of a leader, scowled and took a tentative step forward, as though to impede them, but Jenson elbowed the man aside. When the lot of them were left behind, Johnny Logan felt a definite twinge of relief.

More time must have passed than he realized, while he sat brooding in that jail cell. The afternoon had dragged out and was building toward evening, with sunset not too far away and the light taking on the golden quality it has at that time of day. The town, already abnormally crowded with the influx of boomers, was even busier now as the Saturday trade arrived from nearby ranches — wagon teams standing at the hitch rails, new groups of horsemen constantly arriving off the trails that led into the town like the spokes of a wheel. Boots tramped the walks, and Johnny Logan and his boss were jostled by passersby, when they halted to let Arne Jenson dig out his brier and tobacco pouch.

The cowman had shoved the bundle of Johnny's holster and gunbelt under his arm, and now he filled the pipe bowl, tamping rough cut down with a broad thumb. "It was generous," he grunted, "but I can't see you had any call offering to pay Howbert for that calf."

"I just thought it might help cool him off. After all, *somebody* owes him."

"You going to shoulder the debts for the entire Cheyenne Nation?" the cowman retorted. "On a cowhand's pay?" Before the other could answer, Jenson looked back towards the jail, and Johnny Logan heard him swear under his breath. Johnny saw that "Judge" Rawls had come out, and the others quickly clustered about him for news.

"Look at the self-serving bastard!" Arne Jenson muttered. "He's got that crowd eating out of his hand! Him and his 'newspaper crusade' — I don't see how anybody could be fooled. The man's ambition is to see a white settler on every quarter section of that Cheyenne reservation, and every one of them a vote to help Nate Rawls with his dream of getting back into politics."

Deeply troubled, Johnny Logan asked, "Do you think it'll happen?"

"Well, there's a lot of pressure growing — and Rawls is the blowoff point. Something like this business today can only make things worse. Every time someone like Dallas Howbert gets stirred up, the pressure increases." He shoved the pipe between his teeth, and fished for a match in the pocket of his unbuttoned vest. "I don't know, Johnny. At the moment it don't look good for your people."

Johnny was silent a while as he considered that. "Anyhow," he said finally, "I have to thank you for what you did. I know it put you out on a limb, vouching for me to show up when the law says. I hope you know I won't let you down, Mr. Jenson."

The other man cocked an eyebrow at him, above the match flame cupped in his hand. Blue smoke spurted, and Jenson shook out the match. "If you'd ever given me reason to doubt it," he pointed out dryly, "you'd still be sitting in there . . . But, I ain't too much worried. Like I told the sheriff, it would set worse with me to have a good man drawing his wages and roosting in jail just when I need him.

"Meanwhile," he went on, indicating the gun and belt he held under his arm, "I think it'd make the sheriff feel better if I was to hang onto this. I tell you what. I'm having supper at the hotel. I'll leave your gun at the desk, and you can pick it up whenever you're ready to leave town."

Johnny started to say, "I'm leaving right now," but he was interrupted by someone calling his name. He

32

looked around to see Bob Early and another Bar J hand named Dick Stubbs crossing the busy street. By that time Arne Jenson was already moving on toward the big square of the hotel building, still carrying Johnny's holstered six-shooter. The latter decided he might as well let the matter go for now, and turned to wait for the two Bar J punchers to join him on the sidewalk.

Bob Early caught him by an arm. Early was an earnest fellow, about Johnny's age; just at the moment his mouth was grim beneath the straggle of straw-yellow growth that he was trying to develop into a mustache, and his pale eyes flashed excitement as he exclaimed, "Johnny! For Christ sake, what's going on? Is Dallas Howbert trying to make out you been slow-elking his beef?"

"He's got a carcass hanging on a spike, downstreet in front of the harness shop," Dick Stubbs put in. He was older, with a face that was weather-whipped nearly as dark as Johnny Logan's. "He tells a yarn involving you and one of them reservation Cheyenne . . ."

"I can't blame Howbert," Johnny told them, "for being worked up, seeing one of his steers butchered. Anybody would be. I guess I can even see him not understanding that I knew nothing about it, and got mixed up in the thing by accident. But it's the honest truth."

"If you say so," Early declared emphatically, "then that's good enough for me! So what if the Cheyenne are stealing beef? You ain't responsible."

"That's right!" Dick Stubbs agreed.

It was warming to hear their words. Inwardly Johnny Logan thanked them, but he wasn't entirely reassured. Standing there on the walk with the flow of Saturday afternoon traffic about them, he listened to the pair of them talk but registered little, because Bob Early had raised a troubling question in his mind.

It was easy enough to claim no responsibility for the people on the reservation — it was no way his fault that fate, or accident, had thrown his lot among white men, had given him an upbringing and education that let him hold his own, on at least something like equal terms, in the white man's world. All the same he felt a sudden pang of guilt. Though Johnny Logan's own way wasn't an easy one, it gave him advantages far beyond those kinfolk of his — penned up, trying to hold on to some remnant of their own culture, never allowed to forget they had been beaten and humiliated, and existed now on the charity of their conquerors.

This incident today, involving Badger, proved that something was going on that he ought to have known about. He blamed himself that he hadn't.

He was jarred out of such thoughts by an impatient exclamation from Dick Stubbs. "Time's wasting!" the puncher said gruffly. "And I'm dry from the tonsils down. Why don't we step over to the Palace and — ?"

Johnny knew he wasn't supposed to see Bob Early's warning shake of the head. "Too early for serious drinking," Early said quickly. "Personally, I got my mouth all set for something better than cookhouse grub. I'm for seeing what O'Hara's got on the menu. How about you, Johnny?"

34

"I guess, some other time," the latter told him. "I was about to get my horse and start for the ranch."

Bob Early frowned. "Aw, hell!" he protested. "What kind of fun is that? Johnny, I just can't figure you! All the time I've known you, I ain't once talked you in to spending a Saturday night with us in town. Who wants to sit alone in an empty bunkhouse?"

"You want to spend the evening with an Indian?" Johnny countered, meeting the other's look squarely. "One who won't so much as join you in a drink?" Johnny Logan had never made any bones about that. Not even as a joke would he risk testing himself with so much as a drop of the white man's alcohol. And since heavy drinking was a prime pursuit of all the men he knew and worked with, this refusal of his only helped increase the distance between them.

But Bob Early insisted. "Don't talk loco! Nobody says you have to take a drink. You're with friends — and since you're already here, you got no excuse not to stick around awhile. Johnny, please!"

He was obviously in earnest, and Johnny Logan wavered. But Dick Stubbs remained silent, and Johnny knew from his look that the older man wasn't all that enthusiastic. From hints he'd dropped and from the way he sat a saddle, Johnny was almost sure Stubbs had served a hitch or two in the frontier cavalry. If so, that meant he had fought and killed Indians and watched his comrades killed by them. And a man didn't forget a thing like that. He would work alongside Johnny Logan — and he could even be indignant over seeing him

**35**

jailed on a trumped-up charge; but further than that he might not be ready to go.

Johnny Logan's mouth firmed. "Thanks all the same, Bob," he said. "But I reckon —" And then he saw a group of men making directly for them.

Leading them, Dallas Howbert looked white with anger and thoroughly roused. He was talking loudly before he came to a halt, and a knot of curious passersby began to form as he demanded, "What does this mean? I left you locked in a cell. How did you get out?"

The puncher named Chris, standing beside his boss, scowled and dropped a hand near to his holstered gun. It was Dick Stubbs who, seeing the move, warned sharply, "Before you do anything foolish, you'd better check. The sheriff turned him loose."

"The hell he did!" Chris exploded.

"You don't have to take our word," Bob Early retorted. "You can ask Gifford. Or Mr. Jenson."

"So Jenson stuck his nose in!" Dallas Howbert fixed a bitter stare on Johnny. "I guess I shouldn't be surprised. That's the way it goes with this fellow. One Indian-lover raised him, and another one is taking care of him now."

"That's a hell of a thing to say!" Bob Early began indignantly.

Johnny Logan cut him off. "Let it alone, Bob," he said.

The hatred staring at him from the other man's eyes filled him with dismay. He didn't judge Howbert to be a bad man or a vindictive one. The depth of the

36

rancher's feeling now was an indication of the way emotions had been frayed by events — or rumors of events — in recent weeks. Facing him, Johnny kept his own voice level. "I ain't going to fight with you, Mr. Howbert," he said bluntly. "The sheriff will tell you I've even offered to pay for that calf."

The rancher gave a snort. "So you figure to *buy* your way out of this?"

"You're entitled to your opinion of me," Johnny told him. "But it's up to the judge to decide if I've done anything to be punished for. Meanwhile I've given my word to be here if I'm called to stand trial, and Arne Jenson is pledged to see that I do. Long as the sheriff was satisfied with that, I guess there ain't much you can do about it."

For a moment he thought the man was going to hit him. Dallas Howbert lifted a hand, clenched into a bony fist, but then he let it drop again. His thin lips twisted, and he said in a hoarse voice, "I'll give you some free advice, Logan. This here is a white man's town. We never have let them reservation Indians hang around the streets. And if you got good sense, you'll take the hint. I guess you know what I mean."

"I guess I do," Johnny Logan answered through tight jaws. And Dallas Howbert, without another word, walked on by, brushing past the three from Bar J with his men at his heels.

The curious who had gathered to hear this exchange began to break up when they saw it was over. They left Johnny Logan with fists clenched and cold anger in every tense muscle. Bob Early exclaimed, "Johnny, I don't know who he thinks he is! He had no right to say a thing like that. He —"

Johnny, who had heard scarcely a word the other was saying, cut him off with a new, harder note in his voice: "You mentioned something about O'Hara's. I'm ready to eat whenever you are."

It took a moment for this to sink in. Then Bob grinned widely and clapped his friend on the shoulder. "Good boy, Johnny! Show 'em nobody's going to order you out of this town or any other. You've got as much right here as anybody. Let's get down to O'Hara's while he still has some grub left . . ."

The restaurant was buzzing with trade, but they were lucky enough to find a table somebody had just vacated. They helped themselves to chairs, pushed back the dirty dishes and hung their hats on the floor beside their boots. The waitress who came to clear away the wreckage and swab down the oilcloth gave Johnny Logan a sharp, confused look. No doubt O'Hara normally refused to serve Indians. Johnny, still smarting from the encounter with Howbert, simply stared her down; and then Bob Early stepped in to give his own order, and the woman must have decided not to make an issue. She slapped down silverware, filled their water glasses and left. Early caught Johnny Logan's eye and gave him a grin and a nod. After a moment the latter grinned back, his angry mood easing a little.

The food, when it finally arrived, was just about what they would have had in the cookshack at Bar J — beans and beef and biscuits, and coffee full enough of chicory to lift the roof of your mouth. But just eating it in different surroundings made it taste better; and, listening to the banter of his friends and the lively, boisterous cowboy-talk around him, Johnny Logan found himself begin to relax. Early and Dick Stubbs ribbed one another in cowboy fashion; they deliberately kept away from mention of the difficulties with Dallas Howbert.

The three of them gobbled their food. No cowboy ever ate a leisurely meal, even on his day off. Grabbing their hats, they left money on the table and tramped outside. An orange sun hung swollen above the blue line of hills to the west. At the boomer camp on the flat near town, smoke lifted from supper fires; and along Main Street the dust, stirred by hoofs and wheels, made a golden glitter in the air.

The three cowboys cruised Main Street, part of the ritual of an evening on the town. It was a bare four blocks long. With no purpose they rang their spurs along the sidewalk to one end of it, where the buildings quit and the street played out into a wagon road; here they stood awhile, listening to the noisy town behind them and surveying the open rangeland beyond, as though they had never seen it before.

Shadows of tree and brush stretched long, and the sunset wind brought odors of summer-cooked grass, breathing against their faces. A couple of horsemen shaped up on the road, coming in at an easy lope, and the three punchers speculated idly as they watched them grow larger in the smear of sunset glow. As was usual with stockmen, they studied the horses rather than the riders, and it was Dick Stubbs who said finally, in triumph, "Brady — the one on the left. That's his sorrel."

Bob Early nodded solemnly. "You're right. Other one must be that new foreman of his — what's his name?"

"Clayt Gannon."

"Yeah. I don't like that one. Any idea why Warren Brady should all of a sudden hire him a range boss? He's always handled everything himself."

"Gannon carries the title," the older puncher said with a shrug, "but I sort of think, from the look of him, he's more like a gunhand than a range boss. And I'd say as much about the extra crew he brung with him when he hired on. I understand it all has to do with "Judge" Rawls and that boomer crowd. Brady don't fancy such riffraff pouring in; Gannon's supposed to remind them to keep their distance . . ."

So the idle talk ran on, and Johnny Logan was content to half-listen to his friends gossip, enjoying the rare moment of companionship and nearly able to forget the unpleasant things that had happened to him earlier.

The riders who had been the subject of speculation came on at the same easy lope. The man on the sorrel was, indeed, Warren Brady, owner of a ranch second in size only to Arne Jenson's Bar J among the cattle outfits of this area. Brady didn't much look the part of a successful rancher. He could have been a middle-aged clerk or lawyer, a cleanshaven, petulant-looking man, small of stature, with a weak chin and rimless spectacles. The high-crowned Stetson he favored helped give a false impression of size. And he sat the saddle like a big man, head lifted, not deigning to look at anyone he passed.

Perhaps he relied on the one beside him to act as his eyes. Johnny Logan had heard of this newly hired foreman, but it was the first time he had seen Clayt Gannon. The man was loosely-hung, big-jointed, but there was a hint of strength about him. He had a big nose and an aggressive jaw, and his eyes seemed to take in everything. They rested on Johnny Logan briefly, and the latter felt their chill weight. He had an instinctive feeling that this was someone to be reckoned with, especially by anybody who thought B Cross beef, or range, might be easy pickings . . .

The riders swept past into the town, gritty dust settling behind them, and, having exhausted all the interest at this end of the street, the three punchers turned with one accord and ambled back the way they had come. When they drew opposite the hotel, they saw Clayt Gannon again, still in the saddle, holding the reins of his employer's sorrel horse, while Warren Brady stood on the veranda in conversation with Arne Jenson. It was to be expected the two most important stockmen on that part of the range would have things to talk about when they happened to meet.

Unalike as they were, the two men represented a force in this country that any boomer — or "Judge" Rawls or the law itself — would have to take into account.

The three punchers started again on their aimless tour of the town — "Seeing the sights" — but a voice he overheard caused Johnny Logan to halt and turn his head sharply: "Stamper, who's the short feller there talking to Jenson?"

Like the men from the cow ranches, the boomers apparently stuck together in groups, the two factions seemingly trying to ignore each other. Now a half dozen of these strangers had emerged through the wide double doors of a general store, a couple of them carrying purchases, and one a half-empty whiskey bottle. Perhaps they were celebrating too. They were looking across the street, towards the hotel gallery. Stamper, it appeared, was the red-beard Johnny had noticed earlier, the one he had instinctively picked out as a leader because of his size and a certain aggressiveness in his manner. At least it was he who answered the question, now, while rusty brows drew down over sultry, narrow eyes. "That's Warren Brady," he said gruffly.

"Brady? *That* runt?" the first man echoed. "Hell, I've heard plenty about him since I lit here. But he don't look like much."

"He don't have to look like much," Stamper retorted, "when he owns as much of this country as he does."

Someone else spoke up angrily. "Him and Jenson! Look at the two of 'em! You can see who thinks they're the big roosters in *this* henyard! 'Judge' Rawls says, with any kind of backing from them, we'd of had this reservation business all settled long before this. No such luck, when Jenson even has one of them stinkin' Injuns on his payroll . . ."

The voices broke off. Suddenly Johnny Logan had been discovered on the walk below the porch stoop; scowls beat against him as he stood rooted, fighting a wild impulse to mount the steps and confront the lot of them. His hands were drawn into fists, but he forced himself to calm, telling himself, *This is no good!* These men had been drinking, they were short tempered from the frustration of days spent fruitlessly waiting for the fulfillment of "Judge" Rawls' predictions and of the promises of free homestead land that had lured them here. Johnny Logan had the sense to guess that the wrong word from him now could precipitate real trouble.

He had to remember his debt to Arne Jenson. He couldn't do anything that would cause embarrassment to his employer. So he swallowed his resentment, favored the men on the porch with a final chill look and deliberately turned his back, to join his own companions.

They had gone on without him, apparently unaware of what was happening behind them. They halted in front of a saloon that was already blazing with kerosene lights against the approach of evening; they seemed to be arguing. As Johnny Logan came up, he was in time to hear Stubbs saying angrily, "Look! I'm here to have fun. It sure ain't gonna happen at *this* rate. Is it any of our fault that he —?" And then he broke off, his dark face coloring as both men turned, suddenly aware of Johnny's presence.

Johnny said, without preamble, "Fellows, I'm leaving."

Bob Early exclaimed anxiously, "Look Johnny! We never —"

"That's all right," Johnny Logan assured him. "I know I don't belong here. And I got a feeling, if I hang around, there's going to be more trouble. Myself, I've had enough for one day." He looked from one to the other, trying to judge whether he had persuaded them that his decision had nothing to do with them. He hoped so, because he didn't feel he had much persuasion left in him. "See you at the ranch," he said, and with a nod he walked on and left them standing there.

He remembered that his gun would be waiting for him at the desk of the hotel; but the livery stable was closer. He would saddle up, stopping long enough to pick up the weapon and holster belt on his way out of town. He walked into the barn, which was already dusky with night shadow, though the last light of evening still glowed in the street outside.

He stood a moment to listen to the sounds of horses moving in the stalls, munching at the hay in their mangers, an iron shoe occasionally stomping or striking a timber. The night stable man should be around soon to get a lantern going, but there was no sign of him at the moment. Enough grainy half-light remained to see what he was doing, however, and Johnny Logan went back along the center aisle, checking the stalls. They were all filled, stock saddles and gear racked on the partitions between. Not knowing where his bay had been placed, he had to look into each stall. He finally located the right one, toward the rear of the long aisle.

He gave the animal a slap on the rump in greeting and then eased into the narrow box. He found the blanket and spread it in place. He was just reaching to lift down his saddle when movement at the front end of the building caught a corner of his eye.

Johnny's head whipped up in time to see the figures of two men silhouetted briefly against the gray square of evening light. They came in fast, edging into the black corner beside the wide entrance. Immediately a third one followed, crossing to the opposite side of the opening. Any sound they made had been covered by the noise of animals crowding the stalls. If he hadn't happened to look up at the moment he did, he would have missed the stealthy entrance entirely.

Tensed, he listened, but there was no sound from those others; they must be waiting in the shadows, listening too. All at once he was sure he knew who they were, and alarm and then anger went through him. At the same moment he realized that he was still holding the heavy saddle. Carefully, as soundlessly as possible, he eased it back onto the timber partition.

Despite his care, a stirrup iron swung and struck the wood. The metallic sound was sharp and distinct in the stillness.

As he caught his breath, someone exclaimed by the door in a loud stage whisper: "*Back there!*" Cold sweat broke out on Johnny Logan's ribs.

# CHAPTER
# FOUR

Now that it was too late, he had a solemn moment to remember with regret the six-shooter waiting for him at the hotel desk up the street. He could just as easily have gone there first, before coming here to get his horse; that way at least he would have been armed and able to defend himself.

Johnny Logan stood with the smells and sounds of the horses all around him and watched that square opening of the street entrance, while he tried to guess what was going on up there. He thought they might be chary about coming at him down the center aisle, where they would be clearly silhouetted against the light. They could hardly be sure that he was completely weaponless. But there was another way to get at him, if they wanted to: a storage area and a narrow passage beyond the line of stalls, to his left. They probably knew about that, and there was nothing to keep them from using it.

He had to forget about his horse. He slipped out of the stall, loose straw slithering under his boots, and faded back toward the adjoining stall. Here on the partition was another saddle; Johnny ran a hand over it, thinking he might find a filled rifle scabbard. Nothing

. . . He kept retreating, working toward the back of the barn, and vainly checking each saddle in turn. He began to get a little desperate. Even a pitchfork or other tool might be of some use in self-protection, but he was still empty-handed when he reached the rough rear wall and put his back to it.

His shoulder touched something that he recognized as the loft ladder snaking up the wall to a black hole in the ceiling; he rejected that. If someone was coming after him, he didn't intend to get trapped in a haymow.

Still there had been nothing further from the shadowy figures he had clearly seen sneaking in through the front entrance, and he frowned in puzzlement, wondering what they could be up to. In almost the same breath, it occurred to him that he might be able to guess. Moving past the ladder cleated to the wall, he felt his way along the rough boards until his searching fingers located the edge of a door set into the wall. He had almost forgotten that the barn had a rear entrance; but if his enemies remembered, it might explain why they were waiting.

Hardly breathing, he felt over the surface of the door. It was fastened by a crude latch. Johnny lifted it cautiously, and a hinge creaked. And then, as he tensed to push the door open, he heard sounds from the other side — a boot on gravel, the hoarse breathing of someone just beyond the panel. He was too late. Whoever had been sent around to the back of the barn, to trap him, had got there and was in position.

A moment only he hesitated; then Johnny Logan's jaw set hard. From the loudness of that other breathing, the man must be close behind the door, perhaps even now reaching for the latch. With quick purpose, Johnny set both palms against the panel, and the whole weight of his body went into the shove that flung it wide.

The door was flimsy enough, only one board thick, but it had force behind it and struck its target solidly. Johnny Logan felt the jar as it connected, and thought he heard a grunt of pain. He slammed against it a second time. The obstruction fell away and the door sprang wide enough for him to slip through, and he lost no time doing so.

A man crouched on hands and knees in the cinders. He looked fuddled, as though the door might have caught him in the face hard enough to daze him. He was, Johnny recognized instantly, one of the group of boomers he had seen in front of the general store. A broken bottle lay beside him, and from the dark puddle of moisture soaking into the ground rose the sour smell of cheap whiskey. If he had a gun, Johnny could see no sign of it, and he couldn't spare the time to look. A startled outburst of voices broke inside the barn, and he knew those within would quickly be coming after him.

He turned and began to run.

To his left, on the open spread of brushy ground behind the town itself, lay the boomer camp — ghostly wagons, their canvas lit to a cherry glow by cookfires that sent streams of sparks toward a sky that was now the color of beaten steel. People moved about and dogs barked, and Johnny Logan knew there was nothing in that direction for him. Instead he kept to the rear of the line of buildings, boots spurting gravel as he looked

48

anxiously for a place to hide or a way to lose his pursuers.

He could hear the angry shouting behind him and, he thought, *Why me? What am I to that crowd?* But even as he asked the question, he thought he knew the answer. Those men were bored and disgruntled, waiting for the miracle of free land that had been promised them but so far hadn't materialized . . . and, more than likely, they were drunk. Here was a diversion. It probably didn't even matter that Johnny Logan was Arne Jenson's friend, and therefore could be blamed for Jenson's refusal to throw his weight behind the move to destroy the Cheyenne reservation. It would be enough that Johnny was an Indian.

These men would have to hate all Indians, since you were bound to hate someone you meant to rob. And Johnny happened to be the only Indian in sight at the moment. He would serve their purpose.

It occurred to him that his best chance was to lose himself in the Main Street crowd, and at the next building corner he swung accordingly in that direction. But he braked immediately, because in that instant someone had stepped into the forward end of the opening and, seeing him, raised a shout in warning. Johnny Logan quickly back-pedaled out of the slot, turned and lunged past the corner of the next building. Of a sudden he was really alarmed. Drunk or not, those men were organized and determined to run him down; and it wasn't likely that anyone else in this town, on a lively and crowded Saturday evening, had the slightest inkling of what was going on.

Still following the line of buildings, his heart beginning to pound with the start of panic, Johnny Logan hauled in abruptly. Just before him lay an empty lot and, beyond that, the skeleton of a new building someone was putting up — nothing more than a floor, a framework of timbers, a few stacks of sawn lumber sitting about. The silhouette of walls and roof looked like black pencil strokes. Dusk was closing fast, but enough light remained to see him plainly if he tried to cross those ninety feet of open.

He could hear his pursuers coming up behind; there was no choice. Johnny Logan drew a breath and broke from the protection of the building corner.

Out there in the open he felt lonely and exposed; his legs kept pumping, but the distance seemed hardly to diminish. Suddenly he was alone no longer. They seemed to be coming after him from every direction — from the alleyway, from the street — and already yelling with triumph. His shoulder muscles bunched, half expecting someone to punch a bullet after him; but they didn't seem to be in a gun-shooting mood.

And then, glancing over his shoulder, in grainy dusk he saw the rider. From his black shape, topped by a derby, Johnny thought the man was Stamper — he must have helped himself to a mount he'd found tied to a hitch pole. He was plainly no kind of a horseman. Elbows and knees projected at awkward angles, and it seemed a wonder that he kept the saddle at all. Still he had managed to get the animal into a run. The ground shook to the pounding of its hoofs, and as it bore down on him, Johnny Logan dug in for a last effort to make

**50**

the dubious protection of the house frame, or one of those stacks of lumber.

By now he could hear the breathing of the horse. Suddenly something struck the side of his head and knocked the hat from it. A rope! Stamper had found it on the saddle. Johnny glanced back and saw the horse looming directly over him, and the rider preparing to try again — not whirling the loop, as a cowman would, but simply dabbing it awkwardly toward his quarry's head. With an arm flung up to ward it off, Johnny Logan attempted to change directions.

Not quick enough! Stamper made a lucky cast and the loop settled and as it pulled tight about his throat, trapped the upraised hand as well. Helpless, he was jerked backward, slamming the ground on his shoulders and butt. And then the horse was dragging him through dirt and wood chips and sawdust, while the world seemed to spin crazily, and overpowering smells of dust and pine resin filled his nostrils.

He brought up hard against a pile of lumber. There was a bustle all around him, and angry voices shouting. And then one voice that he almost recognized, saying, "Don't think I won't use this! Now, damn you, back away!"

As things began to settle, he found the strength to push up to a sit. As he did so, someone laid hold of the rope and whipped it free. Cold air filled his throat. A hand caught him under the armpit, and with its aid he climbed to his feet and leaned shakily against the stack of lumber.

A crowd was assembling. Full dusk had settled now, but someone had a lantern, and its streaky light showed Bob Early's angry face and the gun that he leveled while he steadied Johnny Logan with his free hand. It showed, too, the red-bearded Stamper — down off his borrowed horse and glaring, narrow-eyed but careful, into the muzzle of the weapon pointed at him.

"What were you trying to do?" Early demanded. "*Kill* him?"

"Oh, hell!" the boomer leader grunted with a shrug. "That's crazy! We were only playing a little joke on your Injun friend . . ."

Something in his answer snapped the controls on Johnny Logan's temper. Hardly thinking, he lunged forward and drove his right fist into the center of that bristling red beard.

He was shakier than he knew and the blow lacked steam. Stamper was startled by the unexpectedness of it, but he managed to scramble away, not much hurt, though he trampled on the boots of the friends ranged in back of them. There was a moment's confusion while they yelled and scrambled clear, and Johnny had a chance to steady himself. Red anger still controlled him. He was scarcely aware of the shouting voices around him, or of anything else but the face of the man who had roped and dragged him. The face was still there, and he went after it.

There was no question he was the better fighter, in better condition. Stamper, in his forties perhaps, was tough but no match for a younger opponent. He managed to set his boots and slow Johnny for an instant with a blow on the ear that made his whole head ring. But Johnny was too angry to be stopped. He plowed ahead, sank a fist into Stamper's windpipe, and a second later clouted him on the jaw with a force that made the derby pop off the man's head. Stamper gave ground after that, though flailing blows that sometimes hurt but not enough. Johnny Logan forced him back and back, the fight surging across a litter of wood chips and lumber scraps, the yelling crowd flowing with it. Stamper's nose went, with the suddenness of a squashed tomato, and Johnny's knuckles felt the warm gush of blood.

Suddenly he was punching empty air and realized his opponent was down, rolling helpless at his feet.

He held up, panting. He waited with fists ready, but Stamper showed no eagerness to get up and resume the fight. Still blinded by anger, Johnny put up a trembling hand to push the coarse black hair out of his sweaty face. He felt something under his boots, looked down and realized it was his own hat he was trampling. He picked it up and looked at the battered object as though he wasn't entirely clear what to do with it.

The excited crowd still milled around, most of them probably with little idea of what was actually going on. The one with the lantern had been left behind during the fight; now he caught up and the light was shoved without warning into Johnny's face and almost blinded him, making him duck and lift an arm to shield his eyes. But now, into this confusion, a new force intruded itself. It was the sheriff, Zach Gifford, who came wading through the crowd and wedged a way for himself with his gross bulk, as he bellowed questions in an angry roar. When he saw Johnny Logan and the dazed man still sprawled at his feet, the lawman swore loudly and dropped a heavy hand on the young fellow's shoulder.

"You again! I warned you . . ."

Bob Early was there, to protest before Johnny could find his voice. "Let him alone!" the puncher cried indignantly. "Wait at least till you learn the score, before you decide who to get tough with! This wasn't Johnny's doing."

The sheriff turned ponderously to scowl at him. "And what do *you* know about it?"

"I was with him — Dick Stubbs and me, and all minding our own business. He told us he'd decided to ride on out to the ranch, and he went to get his bronc from the livery." Early indicated the boomers, a couple of whom were getting the red-bearded Stamper to his feet. "Dick and me noticed some of this crowd go into the barn, right after him. Before we could even guess what they was up to, they had chased him out here, and they put a rope around his neck, and they was draggin' him."

Gifford still held Johnny by a shoulder. Peering at him, he demanded sharply, "Is that your version?"

Johnny nodded, and Bob Early challenged hotly, "Let them try to deny it!" But the boomers gave back only a sullen silence. Stamper was trying to staunch the flow from his shapeless and swollen nose. Zack Gifford looked the bunch of them over, and with a shake of his

54

massive head let his hand drop from Johnny Logan's shoulder.

"Hell!" he said in high disgust. "I don't know how anyone expects me to do my proper job, and keep the damn town quiet, too! Take him and clean him up," he told Stamper's friends. "Make me any more trouble, and I'll jail the lot of you!" After that he turned to the crowd, flapping his arms at them as though he were shooing chickens. "Get! Break this up! The show's over . . ."

Stamper was led away by his cronies, stumbling and streaming blood. "Come on!" Bob Early said under his breath, holstering his gun. He and Johnny slipped out of the circle of light and grotesque shadows cast by the lantern, vanishing into the confusion of milling men.

Night had fallen by now; stars speckled the black sky, and the fires of the boomer camp were spots of brightness on the wide plain that surrounded the town's lamplit buildings. They stopped while Johnny Logan punched some shape into his trampled headgear and pulled it on, and Bob Early asked anxiously, "You all right?"

There was a tender place toward the back of Johnny's skull, and the knuckles of his right hand hurt when he bent them — a satisfactory reminder of the solid blows he'd dealt Stamper. "No damage," he said. "Thanks for stepping in — and for telling that sheriff the facts. He wouldn't have needed much excuse to jail me again."

"A friend's a friend," Early said gruffly. "You'd of done the same for me." He added on a different note,

"What the hell got into them people, you reckon — to send them after you like that? You hadn't done nothing to them! It looked to me like a lynching!"

"I reckon they were drunk enough," Johnny said. "They didn't really need any reason. I was just handy."

"What are you going to do now?"

He shrugged. "What I started to — get my gun and my bronc and head for home." He added grimly, as the noisy hubbub of the town flowed about them, "I've seen this town now on a Saturday night. I got a feeling it's enough to last me . . ."

Arne Jenson was in a dangerous mood as he entered the Palace nearly an hour after the fight. He had heard some rumor of the disturbance in the town, had dismissed it as the usual Saturday night sort of thing and paid no attention until news finally reached him that Johnny Logan was mixed up in it. That alarmed him and sent him to investigate — but too late. The fight was over, the crowd mostly broken up and scattered. There was no sign of Johnny. He stopped several men, asking questions but getting mixed answers that told him nothing. Then the sheriff's name was mentioned, and he followed that clue to the office of the jail, where he cornered Zack Gifford and, at last, got the story from him.

Even that took some prodding, for the sheriff was full of his own grievance against this town and its eighty-year-old marshal, who should have handled the disturbance. The old man never showed up when he was needed, leaving it for the sheriff to keep the peace

— a task that was no part of a county officer's official duties. Jenson managed, though, to pry most of the facts about the run-in between Johnny Logan and the boomers, and left Gifford grumbling to himself. For his own part, he was considerably alarmed by the news of what had happened.

He had never taken seriously the poaching charges against the Cheyenne, thinking the reports exaggerated and perhaps even invented by Rawls for his newspaper campaign. He'd doubted that the campaign would have any effect, or that there was really any danger to the reservation. As for the throng of boomers, they seemed to him mere riffraff who would soon grow discouraged with fruitless waiting and go chase some other rainbow. But he couldn't discount the violence they had done to Johnny Logan — any more than he could overlook the evidence of actual poaching, by at least one reservation Cheyenne, that Dallas Howbert had turned up today. There was more potential danger here, apparently, than he'd imagined.

He had no idea, of course, of finding Johnny Logan in a saloon, but he thought Bob Early, or even Dick Stubbs, might fill him in on the further details of Johnny's troubles. But neither was in the Palace when he walked in and stood at the slotted doors, surveying the noisy, low-ceilinged room asplash with lamplight. Through the crowd he could see Warren Brady and his new range boss, the tough-looking and seldom-speaking Clayt Gannon, seated at a table toward the rear of the room with a bottle and glasses between them. He was about to go back there when he noticed, at the bar, "Judge" Rawls together with three of his boomer friends.

The man named Stamper was conspicuously absent, but there was enough reason to send Arne Jenson directly toward them, temper showing in his craggy face and in the voice that sheared across other sounds and brought him quick attention.

"Rawls!"

The man jerked about. Jenson came to a stand before him. The talk around them died abruptly and an eddy of stillness began to work through the room; drinks and card games were quickly forgotten. Ignoring the rest, Jenson fixed his angry stare on the gaunt face and beady eyes of the newspaperman. "Rawls," he said again, "it went too far tonight. I don't want to hear of anything remotely like this happening again — ever!"

If he expected the man to be intimidated, he was mistaken. Rawls returned his stare, mouth drawn down over his rabbity teeth in a look of sour defiance. The three boomers, an odd assortment, were absolutely motionless; they seemed to be holding their breath.

Now Rawls told the rancher crisply, "I suppose you're talking about your Indian friend getting himself roughed up a little while ago. Blame yourself for that, Jenson! You should have left him in that cell where he belonged — then nothing would have happened to him."

"He has as much right on the streets of this town as anybody!"

One of the boomers, a black-haired hulk of a fellow in soiled overalls, seemed unable to hold back. "Not a dirty redskin!" he burst out. "Not in a white man's town."

Arne Jenson turned to favor him with a cold, appraising look. "Were you one of them that tried to kill him?"

"There was no thought of killing," "Judge" Rawls said quickly. "The boys have been telling me, the idea was just to teach him a needed lesson."

Jenson skewered him with a look. "I take it you don't want anyone getting the idea *you* were involved . . ."

"Because I wasn't!"

"But you were! From the first rabble-rousing speech you made and the first editorial on the front page of that paper of yours, trying to work people up against the Cheyenne — on no evidence."

"No evidence!" Rawls snapped, his sallow cheeks taking on color. "Just today, your own neighbor — Mr. Howbert — caught them red-handed!"

"Today has nothing to do with the deliberate campaign you've been waging, now, for a month and longer."

"But it proves I was right all along!" the other quickly countered. "Deny that if you can!"

There was no good answer to that. Arne Jenson scowled as a dozen angry replies crowded to his tongue and died there, none of them worth uttering. But Rawls had no chance to savor his triumph, for a new voice spoke now, and they turned to see Warren Brady working his way through the silent crowd to the bar, his foreman just behind him. Men made way for him — somehow you didn't notice his lack of size, and when he spoke, the authority of his voice more than compensated for the ordinariness of his features.

"I got a word to put in here," he said. "With all this talk of poaching, it hasn't happened to the B Cross; but I for one am not depending on newspaper editorials — or even on the sheriff's office — to see that it doesn't. I've taken other steps."

"It's clear enough what steps you mean," "Judge" Rawls answered, and he eyed the silent presence who stood at Brady's elbow. Clayt Gannon returned the look with cool indifference. He didn't seem to mind that the filled holster at his lean thigh labeled him plainly for what he was. "Unfortunately," Rawls said dryly, "not every rancher is prosperous enough that he can afford to hire extra crew — or pay them gun wages."

"That's their misfortune," Brady answered. "I *can*, and I've done it. And my crew has their orders." His spectacles flashed lamplight as he turned his head and looked directly at the boomers.

The one who had spoken earlier demanded aggressively, "Any particular reason you should be looking at *us*, mister?"

"I'll leave that for you to answer," Brady told him. "I'll simply say this: I don't like you people. You're a bunch of would-be land grabbers. And while you wait around for your chance, you've got nothing to keep your hands busy. Well, pass this word to your friends: I'm keeping an eye on the lot of you, and my crew is alerted. You aren't going to grab land from *me*. And if you happen to get hungry for meat, just remember that

B Cross isn't supplying free beef to anyone, be he white or red!"

He waited for no reply but simply turned and walked out, his gunman following him closely. The warning he left seemed to hang in the stillness, even after the bat-wing door had stopped swinging. But after that the hubbub of sound began again, mounting quickly. At the bar "Judge" Rawls' boomer clients fell into intense wrangling among themselves.

Rawls shot an uneasy glance at Arne Jenson, but the rancher wasn't looking. He was busy with the run of his own thoughts — with a feeling that he was only beginning to realize how serious matters had become, almost without his notice.

He hadn't believed the rumors about the Cheyenne, probably because he didn't want to. Now there was proof that the rumors were at least partly true, and suddenly he could foresee nothing at all but trouble.

# CHAPTER
# FIVE

On Sunday Johnny Logan rode from Bar J headquarters toward the Cheyenne reservation. He had strapped his saddle onto his own horse, a good-looking black that he'd had under him when he left Matt Logan's ranch in the Bitterroots and came to this country looking for clues to his own people.

Today he was half consciously hunting a different kind of clue, keeping an eye out for evidence of horses or cattle moving across the reservation boundary. He had no special expertise as a tracker, but he thought that if there were a sign to support a claim that the Cheyenne were working on the beef of neighboring ranchers, he should be able to turn it up. He wasn't particularly surprised when he failed to find anything.

Arne Jenson certainly had had no reports of missing stock, and what they heard from other spreads had been strictly rumor and hearsay — at least until yesterday and the incident involving himself and Badger and Dallas Howbert. *That* was no rumor. That was fact, and it cried out for attention.

The sun was high when he crossed an invisible boundary line onto the three-hundred-and-seventy-thousand-acre tract of land reserved for the Northern

Cheyenne. It was hardly any wonder that men like Stamper were eagerly waiting a chance at them. Free range and choice homestead land, all through the West, having long since been picked over, here was something to make their mouths water. Unlike the kind of worthless scrub that had usually been fobbed off on the defeated Indian tribes, this had been chosen by the Cheyenne themselves. It contained good grass, water, and timber. From the very start, Johnny Logan understood, there had been considerable protest and clamor over its being turned over to the tribes. Now the demands for appropriating it were growing louder with every day that passed — and with every editorial in "Judge" Rawls' newspaper.

Johnny had never visited Lame Elk's village, but he knew where to look for it. Now that the buffalo were gone, the once nomadic people were being slowly forced to adopt the ways of agriculture, and with crops in the ground some villages had acquired very nearly the status of permanent settlements. Johnny Logan followed general directions and presently rode in on a collection of cone-shaped lodges, covered with government-issue canvas instead of buffalo hide and arranged in a wide circle with running water and a few patches of cultivated ground handy. Familiar smells of wood fires and sounds of children yelling, dogs barking and a pony neighing on its picket met him as he neared.

In some dim recess of earliest childhood memories, out of a time before his own family had been massacred by drunken whites, Johnny Logan felt a sense of familiarity and belonging whenever he entered one of

**63**

these reservation villages. Yet because of his divided nature, due to a white upbringing, he found himself repelled by the squalor and poverty of the life he saw here. Once these had been a proud and warlike people. Now they were reduced to nothing and little hope of more. He saw the shoddy equipment, the shapeless issue clothing, the general lack of spirit, and it was enough to make him sick at heart.

He knew only a few words of the Cheyenne tongue, but he reined in to ask directions of a squaw who was bent nearly double under a load of firewood. With gestures he managed to learn from her the location of Badger's lodge.

On a day this warm, the canvas coverings of most of the village tepees were rolled up from the bottom to allow for circulation of whatever cooler air might be stirring, but it was not so with Badger's. The cover was stretched taut over the poles, the door flap was tightly closed, and a pencil-line of blue smoke rose from the opening at the top, where lodge poles bunched against the sky. With sunlight beating on the canvas and a fire burning, it occurred to Johnny Logan that the interior of the lodge must be nearly breathless.

Sounds of a man's voice chanting off-key issued from the tepee. The only other indication of life was a half-grown boy who hunkered, nearly naked, amid the clutter of scattered junk and cold ashes of dead fires before the lodge, absorbed in some mysterious game involving stones and pieces of wood. When Johnny spoke, the head with its black mane of hair whipped up, and the boy stared at him in silence. He tried again, using what Cheyenne words he knew in asking after the whereabouts of the man named Badger. Still without answering, the lad got to his feet, keeping his eyes on the stranger as he backed away and then slid under the tent flap.

Johnny Logan dismounted, dropping the black's reins while he stood listening to the wailing chant within. Abruptly the flap was swept aside, and Badger ducked into view, halting at sight of his visitor. In that instant Johnny was able to see past him to the tepee's interior, glowing with sunlight on canvas. He had a frozen glimpse of a man in breechclout and buffalo headdress, his sweat-glistening body hung with strings of eagle bones and amulets, his upraised hands holding a bone rattle and an eagle feather. At the feet of the medicine man, a motionless human figure lay wrapped in blankets. A glimpse was all Johnny had. Then Badger straightened and let the canvas fall into place behind him, but not before the boy who had summoned him slipped out and scampered away, a swift brown shape that was quickly gone.

Badger's broad face was streaming with sweat, and though the face was carefully expressionless, Johnny was sure the man recognized him. He saw Badger turn his head slightly, black eyes seeking for the rifle that leaned against a stump near the lodge, the same weapon he had carried yesterday when he fled from Dallas Howbert's men. Johnny read his thought and said quickly, "You can leave the gun where it is, Badger."

Slightly slanting black eyes stabbed at Johnny, in a way to let him know that the man knew enough English to understand what he had said. He made no move toward the rifle, and he offered no reply. Johnny asked, "There is sickness in your lodge?"

The flat lips stirred. Speech, when it came, was short and guttural: "My woman and my youngest son. Both with fever. Very bad."

"I'm sorry," Johnny said and meant it. Though the other's face held no hint of emotion, his anxiety showed in the way he stiffened and turned when the toneless chanting within the lodge broke off for a moment. But then the sound resumed, and with it the dry clatter of the rattle and the shuffling of moccasined feet. Badger brought his dull stare back to Johnny's face as the latter continued:

"It's not a good time to be bothering you, but I'm afraid I have to. I suppose you've guessed why I rode over here."

Badger's head tilted in the slightest of nods. "You stop those white men." It was a grudging acknowledgement. "They would kill me, I think. But I watch and see how you make them turn back. Why?"

"Do you have to ask? I thought maybe you knew about me. I'm Johnny Logan. It's a white man's name, but I'm full-blood Cheyenne myself. What I did for you, I'd have done for any other against odds like those. I got into bad trouble because of it, because of you, Badger, and the calf you butchered. Those men wouldn't believe I didn't have something to do with it.

They got me thrown in jail, and I'm still not in the clear."

He paused to see if Badger would say anything, but the man's flat lips were tight set, and his eyes showed no understanding. Anger began in Johnny and made him speak more harshly than he intended.

"I wonder if you have any idea at all," he exclaimed, "how things stand with the Cheyenne right now! We have a few good friends among the whites, but we won't keep them long if you people don't start leaving the ranchers' beef alone! Man, do you *want* to lose the reservation, and see the Cheyenne carted away somewhere?"

The other's face drew into a scowl. "You think Badger kill the steer for himself? Badger's woman and son need meant so they be strong again. Badger meant it for them."

"Was that an excuse to *steal!*" Johnny Logan retorted. "It can't have been that long since ration day. Surely someone in the village had beef to spare your family."

"No beef," the man told him, doggedly shaking his head. "No flour, few damn beans. You look around and see. The people are hungry. Some hunt deer, bear, rabbit. Badger no can take time to hunt. Badger must stay close, help in sickness. But yesterday —" And he shrugged to complete the sentence, leaving Johnny staring at him in slow comprehension.

Badger's manner was that of a desperate man driven to desperate measures. He was telling Johnny that he had dared to butcher one of Dallas Howbert's animals only out of sheer necessity and need for his ailing family. Still the whole thing was incredible, and Johnny pressed him hard: "Do you mean to say, something's happened to the rations you people are supposed to be getting? Since when?"

Badger only shrugged a second time. His broad features had again taken on a look of dull despair, as though he saw no use in further explanations. At that moment there was a sharp cry of suffering from within his lodge. It whipped his head around sharply. A low, animal sound of distress broke from him. Forgetting Johnny Logan, he lumbered about and pawed aside the canvas flap and plunged headlong through the tepee entrance. Johnny was left staring open-mouthed.

Puzzled by what he had just heard, he reached up, took off his hat and ran his fingers through the coarse black hair that hung almost to his shoulders. Pivoting slowly, he looked around him, studying the village with thoughtful eyes, awakened to new possibilities by what Badger had said. It *looked* no more poverty-stricken than these reservation settlements generally did, but that was no sure sign. Even with their plantings of corn and root crops, the Cheyenne were chiefly dependent on the rations issued twice monthly at the Agency, and would feel it sorely if for any reason those were being held up.

For a moment Johnny Logan considered making further enquiries in the village — perhaps finding old Lame Elk, the head chief, and getting confirmation from him. But then he shook his head. Somehow he knew that wouldn't be necessary. There'd been truth in

Badger's outburst. He had stated simple fact. And if Johnny Logan needed to know more, there was a better place than this to look for it.

Quickly determined, he pulled on his hat, caught up ground-anchored reins and swung into the saddle of the black. Starting away from Badger's lodge, he saw the half-grown Cheyenne lad watching him silently and lifted a hand to him in salute.

The boy never moved or even blinked. Johnny kneed the horse into motion. The chanting of the medicine man inside the lodge followed him, muffled and quickly lost in the sound of the black's hoofs carrying him from the village.

Walker Springs Agency consisted of a cluster of log buildings and canvas tepees set against a protecting rise on whose slope, just below where the rim cut against the sky, someone had worked out the initials "W S" in whitewashed stones. Of a Sunday the place showed little activity. Even the United States flag had not been run up on the pole before the main building. Johnny Logan saw no activity around the place at all, but he knew the agent's living quarters were in the rear of the headquarters building, and so he rode on in. Coming closer, he saw that the door stood open behind its screen. He dismounted at a hitching post and gave the leathers a couple of wraps. He went up the low steps and knocked at the door's edge. He heard a gruff command to enter. Johnny Logan pulled open the screen and stepped inside.

A blond, ruddy-faced man of about forty, in shirtsleeves and an unbuttoned waistcoat, frowned at him from the desk where he sat with papers before him and a pen in his hand. He appeared to be trying to make his visitor out against the blaze of sunlight beyond the door. Johnny took a further step into the room, and now the man seemed able to see him more clearly. "I think I know you," he grunted. And then, nodding: "Sure! You're the Indian who works for Arne Jenson, the one that had something to do with getting rid of that crook, Walsh, that had this job before me. They call you Logan, don't they?"

"That's right."

"Well!" Bart Simpson, the Indian agent for Walker Springs, laid down his pen. "Something I can do for you?" His manner remained cautious, potentially hostile.

"It depends," Johnny told him bluntly. "I got a question I have to ask you, Mr. Simpson, and I won't beat around the bush. I heard today that the Cheyenne aren't getting the supplies they got due them. I was told they're actually going hungry. I came to you to find out the truth of it."

The other's eyes seemed to go opaque, and his features became carefully expressionless. He said, "I could tell you it's none of your business, since you have nothing to do with the reservation or with the agency. But I can see you're concerned, and I hardly blame you, I am, myself. These are your people and my job." He made a short gesture toward a chair beside the desk. "You might as well have a seat while we talk it over."

70

Johnny Logan hesitated briefly, then eased onto the chair and placed his hat in his lap. Simpson settled back and regarded him. Johnny returned the look, waiting. To him, this man seemed rough-speaking but reasonably honest — actually, a decent enough sort.

"It'd be a lie to say your friends aren't getting a rotten deal," the agent said bluntly. "Not from *me*, I hope. I'm paid to run this agency as best I can, and I figure it's better for everybody — the white man included — if the Cheyenne can be kept happy."

"So just what is the trouble?"

"I'll be damned if I really know! That's the truth. Somewhere, something's gone wrong. About six weeks ago the flow of rations to the agency began to slow up. Now it's not much more than a trickle of what it should be. I've checked with the other agencies on the reservation, and they've got the same situation. I've complained to higher authorities, and so far I've had no satisfaction. No one seems able to tell me a thing."

"Hard to believe, though, you haven't got some ideas," Johnny Logan said.

The other's eyes blinked with impatience. "Look!" he pointed out shortly. "I'm a pretty small frog, and I haven't been around this particular puddle long enough to know everything that goes on in it! I only know that there's a long chain of command that stretches between this office and the Indian Bureau in Washington. There's some pretty powerful men along that chain. How would I know at what level the ration money is disappearing — or into whose pocket?"

Johnny silently considered this while a tin alarm clock ticked away on a shelf above the desk, and somewhere outside a dog barked a few times and fell silent again. A sense of futility engulfed him, of distant and faceless enemies beyond reach, and he shook his head in bitter admission. "So helpless men and women and children have to pay the penalty . . ."

"Logan," Bart Simpson declared, "all I can tell you is this: I'm raising as much hell over this situation as I know how." He indicated the papers on the desk before him. "I'm writing everyone I can think of, trying to get some action. So far nothing's had any effect; nobody pays me any attention. If there's anything more I could be doing, I wish I knew what it was!"

"All right," Johnny Logan said and rose abruptly to his feet. "I guess you're trying. I'm sorry I bothered you."

He had reached the door when the agent stopped him. "Logan!" Something in his voice made Johnny look back, to see the scowl on his ruddy face. "I've heard you're a scrapper," the agent went on. "I got a feeling you'd like to take this battle on, yourself. Not that I blame you. I'd feel the same way, in your boots. But believe me, it's useless! Whoever's responsible is away beyond your reach, and mine too, or so it appears. I'm sorry, but that's just the way it is."

He paused to see if his words were having any effect; something in Johnny Logan's face must have told him otherwise. He leaned forward, arms on the desk, chair creaking under him. "I only hope you won't try anything foolish . . ."

Johnny stared at him a moment longer in silence. Then, not bothering to answer, he pushed out into the sunshine, headed for his waiting horse. The screen door jangled shut behind him.

He had one other place on the reservation he wanted to visit, and he arrived there with the sun high at noon and shadows shrunken to their smallest. Here were more log buildings — principally the one-roomed school house where Howard Cummings taught the children of the Cheyenne something of their own culture, as well as the reading and writing and figuring, with slate and chalk, of the white men who had conquered their people. This being Sunday, the school was not in use, though there would be religious services later. Cummings, though not himself a minister, operated under the pay and auspices of a church group in the East. Johnny Logan rode directly to the schoolteacher's house nearby.

He was about to knock when the porch door opened unexpectedly, catching him with arm upraised. A girl stood staring at him, and for a moment it might have been hard to say which wore the blankest look of surprise. Johnny was first to recover. He saw how funny they both must look, and he grinned at her. At that the girl laughed, stepped forward and seized both his hands. "Johnny!" she cried. "Oh, Johnny!" And she went on tiptoe to kiss him on the mouth. He slipped his arms around her waist and held her for a moment.

She was a small girl — Cheyenne like himself, her body firm and strong under the simple cotton

73

housedress. Enormous dark eyes, framed by twin braids of raven-black hair, held a luminous warmth of love as she smiled at him. Her name was Crow Wing; but the Cummingses, having adopted her, called her "Anne," and so did Johnny Logan.

"How good to see you," she said, and he felt the warmth of her breath against his throat. "We've missed you. We all have."

"It's been too long," he agreed. "But it's a busy time of year. I helped take some cattle over to Dakota, for Mr. Jenson. We were gone most of a month. And since we got back, I haven't had time to get over to the reservation." He frowned and added, "Maybe I should have *made* the time."

She caught his mood, and her own face quickly grew serious. "Things haven't been good here," she admitted. "But I don't know what you, or anyone, could have done about it . . ."

After that she had his hand again and was leading him into the house, calling out, "Look who's here! It's Johnny Logan!"

The main room, combining sitting room and kitchen and eating space, was simply but comfortably furnished, mostly by the labor of the schoolteacher's own hands. Just now it held the good aromas of roasted chicken and sweet corn and home-baked bread and coffee. Ella Cummings turned from the wood stove, with a bowl of gravy for the table that was set for three.

She was a birdlike little woman with brown hair, slightly graying, drawn neatly back. She smiled a welcome, and now Howard Cummings came in with a welcoming hand extended. Bluff and bearded, he had the look of a blacksmith but was one of the gentlest men Johnny Logan had ever known. Pulling off his hat, Johnny shook hands with him. "It's good to see you," Cummings said. "You're just in time to sit down with us."

"I never meant —" he began in protest, but the big man waved that aside.

"Nonsense! I guess you know where to wash up. Anne, set out another plate . . ."

The food, prepared by Ella Cummings, was plain but delicious. "It's all from our own garden," she explained when Johnny complimented her; and added, with a troubled frown, "Actually, it makes us feel guilty to be eating so well, when we know what's going on around us."

"The problem's just too big," Howard Cummings said darkly. "We can't feed the whole reservation out of our vegetable patch. And besides, these are a meat-eating people. We do what we can, manage at least to get some good food into the children at the school each day. Meanwhile the church group I work for is trying to raise extra funds and shipments of supply, but their best can't go very far."

"Is it only the Cheyenne?" Johnny wanted to know. "Do you know if other reservations are getting this kind of treatment?"

"From what I've been able to learn, this is the only one."

"I talked to Simpson, at the agency." Johnny Logan repeated the gist of that conversation, while the others listened solemnly. Cummings slowly nodded his big head.

"Bart Simpson is a good man, but I doubt there's anything a local agent would have the power to do."

"He says it's a plain matter of graft. What I don't understand," Johnny went on, "is why we haven't heard any rumors. If Mister Jenson still held the beef contract, you can bet, the minute the ration money was cut off, *he'd* have been raising Cain, trying to find out why the Cheyenne were being done out of their meat supply."

The schoolteacher said bitterly, "Nobody really cares! As long as the Indian was able to stand and fight back, the white man had to respect him. Now that he's broken, he's something to be pushed into the corner and forgotten. Otherwise, he might be a burden to someone's conscience."

Anne, listening in silence to all this, suddenly burst out, "Does *any* —?" and then broke off in confusion. Cummings looked at her with his mild brown eyes.

"Does any white man actually have a conscience?" he finished for her. "Is that what you started to say?"

Her dark eyes shone suddenly with tears. "I'm sorry!" she blurted, looking blindly from one to the other of her foster-parents. "I had no right to say that — not to *you!*"

"No call to apologize," Cummings told her kindly, "for saying or even thinking it. With all our Christian talk of forgiveness and charity, no Indian could be blamed for wondering how much of it any of us really means . . ."

76

Sobered, no one spoke for awhile. They ate in silence, and a square of sunlight from a curtained window moved slowly across the table. "So what does a man do," Johnny Logan exclaimed finally, "when he's starving — and maybe his wife and child are ill and need good red meat to help get back their strength?" They all looked at him, questioning, and he added: "You know a man named Badger? In Lame Elk's village?"

"Of course," said Anne quickly, and Cummings added, "Badger's oldest son used to come to school, though we haven't seen him lately. I remember, I've heard him boast that his father is the best tracker on the reservation."

"Is there illness in Badger's family?" Anne wanted to know.

Johnny told them about the medicine man in Badger's lodge, and then he went on to relate the trouble that had arisen over Badger's killing of a steer belonging to a white rancher. Of his own part in the matter, he told only enough to explain how Badger had escaped. The fact that he had been caught up in the trouble and landed in a jail cell, he felt no call to mention.

"The question is," he finished, watching the shocked and troubled faces of his hearers, "how many more of the Cheyenne are being driven to do what Badger did — out of hunger, or maybe just out of revenge? Raiding the ranchers' beef herds can only give ammunition to those who want to close out the reservation and ship the Cheyenne off south to the Indian Nations. Or have you heard *that* talk?"

"Oh, yes!" Cummings said grimly. "I've heard it, all right! And I've read it in the newspaper — though never a word of any kind," he added pointedly, "about conditions on the reservation! But I don't suppose *that's* important enough . . ."

Coffee cup raised to his lips, Johnny Logan suddenly went still and then set the cup down again, working at something that had caught at the edge of his thoughts — almost like the glimpse from the tail of your eye, before the animal you were hunting slunk away in the underbrush.

It might mean nothing at all, but he had the gut-stirring feel that he had hit on something that needed looking into.

# CHAPTER
## SIX

Later Anne walked out to the shed with Johnny, where the black had been enjoying a bait of hay and oats. She watched in silence as he replaced the bit, then led it outside and tightened up the cinch. They stood alone for a moment, with afternoon wind and sunlight setting a row of cottonwoods to twinkling above them.

Anne said wistfully, "I always hate to see you go . . ."

"I always come back, don't I?" he answered, grinning.

"But someday you won't. We both know that, Johnny. Cowboying for Mr. Jenson — that's not enough for you."

"It's a good job," he protested, "and Arne Jenson's been a good boss to work for. Besides, it's not so far from the reservation that I can't get over to see *you* every now and then.

"Still," he admitted, "I know I'll never be able to save anything on a rider's wages, or do the things I want for you and me. And, besides . . ." He hesitated. Her waiting look encouraged him to continue, telling her the thought that had been taking shape in him more and more of late. "There's a lot of world out there — and maybe, if I'm lucky, something I can find to do that will make it possible to help our people. I haven't any idea what, yet. It's no more clear than that, I'm afraid."

"Of course," she agreed quickly. "And I knew that was how you were thinking, even though you never said as much. I understand you well enough by this time, Johnny Logan . . ." But then she fell silent again, and he could tell that something else was troubling her. Remembering the talk at the dinner table, he thought he could guess what it was, and he waited for it to come tumbling out, while her wide black eyes pinned his face.

"Do you suppose there's really a chance of the reservation being taken away and the people shipped back to the Nations? Could they really do it?"

"When white men want something the Indian has," Johnny answered grimly, "they usually find a way to get it. This time? I just don't know!"

"This time, I'm afraid, there's no way the Cheyenne can fight back to hold what's theirs. They haven't much fight left, Johnny! They'll go where they're taken. And they'll die there!" She clutched Johnny's sleeve. It hurt him to see the pain in her eyes, but he couldn't look away from them. "I was only a baby, too little to remember the Nations, but all my life I've heard the old ones tell how bad it was. So far from home, there were diseases in that place they weren't immune to — or if nothing else, they just took sick and died from homesickness. Until, finally, the ones that were left couldn't stand any more of it — until they decided it would be just as well they all were dead. And so . . ."

And so they had just got up and left — all the Northern Cheyenne! Johnny had heard the story from older Indians as well as from Anne, who, even though no more than a toddler then, still had vivid memories of the desperate trek north across Kansas and Nebraska, harried at every step by the white soldiers — trying only to make their way home to Montana. Anne could still remember the hunger and the cold and the fear. Her mother had taken ill and died soon after from the hardship. With all the forces of the white man set to cut them off, and destroy them if necessary, a bare half of those who started the long trail had finally made it through. And after all that punishment, been allowed at last to settle on a reservation of their own choosing . . .

"And now — to go through it again!" Anne exclaimed in a broken voice. "It just can't be, Johnny! There'd be no escape a second time. They'd all die down there. I *know* it!"

Johnny Logan covered her hand with his. "Maybe it won't happen," he said, and thought at once how lame that sounded; but the girl seemed to take some kind of reassurance from his words. At least she managed a smile for him, and Johnny bent and kissed her on the lips. Moments later he turned to steady the stirrup for his boot and swing into the leather.

Anne stepped back, her hands clasped behind her. As he looked down at her from the saddle, she said, "I'll go call on Badger's family — see if there isn't something I can do to help them."

"Good!" Johnny agreed, the reins in his hands. "Frankly, I don't think Badger has much faith in that medicine man."

He lifted an arm in farewell and rode from there. Before he passed into the timber, he looked back. The girl stood where he had left her, watching after him, shielding her eyes against the sun with a wrist.

When he caught sight of the riders, Johnny knew at once that he had also been seen. In these grassy, rolling hills near the reservation boundary, only sparsely timbered, a horseman could easily be spotted by his dust and at considerable distances. The pair he'd seen only briefly were cutting out of a timbered draw and across an open roll of land, on a course that should intercept his own. They were probably as curious about him as he was about them. In such times as these, almost anyone might have business here, or, to look at it another way, no legitimate business at all.

If they were that anxious for a look at him, Johnny didn't feel inclined to avoid it. He had left his belt gun in the bunkhouse that morning, but there was a rifle on his saddle. He saw no particular reason for alarm. Even if these were enemies, he should manage to protect himself.

He saw them next a half mile farther on, where the dimly marked trail he was following dipped around a shoulder of hill and crossed a dry stream bed. There, under the dappling of poplar heads, the riders had pulled up beside the trail and were watching him approach. For just a moment he nearly drew rein, as he saw that one was Clayt Gannon and that the other had the clear look of one of the tough crew he bossed for Warren Brady. They were both armed.

But it was too late to back away from a meeting, and he knew no good reason why he should. They merely sat and watched him come, horses idly switching their tails as a warm wind stirred the poplar branches. Johnny began to think they intended to let him ride by, without a word or move of interference; but with a few yards still separating them, Gannon's companion casually lifted the reins and walked his horse out into the trail, turning him headon to face the newcomer.

To go forward would be to let himself be flanked, and Johnny Logan drew in.

No one spoke as the pair looked him over, Gannon from his position at the side of the trail, the other man facing Johnny. Clayt Gannon spoke. "Yes, I think this is him. I saw him in town last evening."

"It's Logan," the other agreed. "I seen him beat the bleedin' whey out of one of them boomers — fellow they call Stamper."

"And a tough one too, I understand," Clayt Gannon said, nodding.

Johnny Logan was growing angry. He felt that he was being discussed like a steer, or a ham being judged on its points. "For your information," he told them, "Stamper wasn't all that tough. He was out of condition and he was kind of drunk. It wasn't too hard to beat him. Now if we're all satisfied about that . . ." He lifted the reins suggestively, indicating he wanted to ride on.

No one moved to let him by. Clayt Gannon said, "I don't think my friend Mitch is satisfied. Mitch has opinions about an Indian beating a white man with his fists."

"Damn right!" Mitch confirmed gruffly, and Johnny felt himself grow cold.

He knew then that they were deliberately baiting him, that they meant trouble. He thought of the rifle in his scabbard, knew he couldn't get to it before one or both of them had him covered with their belt guns. He made himself return their looks without any expression on his own dark face. Johnny was trying to decide if this was serious, or if it was perhaps some sort of cruel sport these two were having with him.

Clayt Gannon's gaunt face told nothing, but somehow Johnny got the impression that the other man was dead serious. Mitch was a big fellow, with shoulders so heavy with muscle that there seemed to be no neck at all between them and the round, battered-looking head. His face was knobby; the nose had been broken and improperly set. If he had been in the crowd last night that watched the set-to with the man named Stamper, Johnny had been too busy to notice him.

Looking at him now, he could judge that Mitch was a man who put as much store by the weight of his fists as he did by the efficiency of his gun, and there was real anger in him now when he said harshly, "An Indian's a skulker. He comes crawlin' at you out of the dark with a knife in his teeth. I just ain't ready to admit that *any* sneakin' redskin could lick a white man in a fair fight!"

84

Johnny drew a breath. "Ask Stamper if *he* admits it," he suggested shortly. And deliberately he walked his horse forward.

Mitch sat and watched him come, plainly trying to fathom what the other man was up to. Gannon, too, held where he was, at one side of the trail. It was part of Johnny's gamble that he would stay there. His own stare held close on Mitch's scowling face as the black closed the distance. Now, at a slight pressure of the rein, the horse started to swing wide, to move around and past Mitch.

The latter saw what he intended. A curse broke from him, and his left arm shot out and clutched the front of Johnny's denim jacket; his right went for the Colt revolver in his belt holster. Johnny had made no attempt to avoid the other's grip; but now, without warning, he gave a sudden, savage kick with the spur.

The black was only months past being a wild stallion, captured in the foothills of the Bitterroots. Only Johnny Logan had ever succeeded in riding him, and from Johnny he had known nothing but gentleness and consideration. Now the sharp and unexpected bite of the spur had its hoped-for effect. It brought a squeal of anger from the horse and sent it lunging straight into Mitch's animal.

Startled and unnerved by the sudden flash of bared teeth, Mitch lost his hold on Johnny. His own horse flinched aside, for the moment out of control. And Johnny Logan had the chance he needed to aim a clubbing blow at the side of the big man's head. It struck at the point where the almost non-existent neck joined the shoulder, and it had all Johnny's weight and the drive of the lunging black behind it. Mitch's head jerked, the gun popped out of his fingers. He lost his saddle and dropped helplessly between the two lunging horses; he struck the ground hard.

Johnny quickly reined the black aside, to prevent it trampling the downed man. He knew without looking that Mitch was too dazed to be any danger at the moment, so he hunted for Clayt Gannon, at the same time rather desperately reaching for the rifle under his knee. In his haste he got it jammed in the leather, and there it stuck, resisting every hurried effort to pull it free.

And then, with the black still moving around and kicking up the yellow dust, he located Gannon and saw that the gunman had made no move at all. His gun was still in its holster. He looked at Johnny over the sprawled shape of the man stirring feebly on the ground, and Johnny thought there was a faint hint of amusement behind his stare. He said coldly, "I don't know what you proved with that, but I don't think my friend's going to be happy about it."

"What about yourself?" Johnny demanded.

For answer he got no more than a level stare and then, perhaps, the briefest hint of a shrug. He settled for that and shoved the rifle back into its scabbard.

It was as though iron bands around his chest constricted his breathing; Johnny moved his shoulders to ease them. A last look at Mitch, who had pushed himself up to a sitting position in the trail but seemed too fuddled to be aware of what was going on; then he deliberately swung the black and struck out from there at a canter. He let himself relax only when a lift and turn of the trail put that scene under the poplars behind him.

He laid a hand on the black's smooth neck. "Sorry, fella," he said gruffly. "I treated you pretty rough. But I didn't know how else to get out of that . . ."

The encounter had left him keyed up and dry of mouth. He thought of Mitch — those massive shoulders, that bullet head, the weight of the fist that had closed on his jacket and seemed enough to fairly tear it off him. Mitch was not going to forget what had happened back there on the trail. He would be looking for a settlement with the Indian who had dared to dump him off his horse.

It was simply one more thing, among so many, for Johnny Logan to worry about . . .

At his desk in the silent newspaper office, that Monday morning, Nathan Rawls read over the editorial he had just been working on and gave himself an occasional nod or grunt of self-approval for this point well made, that graceful turn of expression. A man with his gift of language, he told himself again, should not be forced to waste it in the columns of an obscure cow-country newspaper like the *Weekly Advocate* of Monroe, Montana. He should be composing speeches for delivery on the floor of the Senate, or well-reasoned judicial decisions to be handed down from some high bench of power — with the nation's flag beside him on its standard and the hushed solemnity of a courtroom lending gravity to the importance of his words.

Well, an ambitious man must learn to wait for his opportunities — or make them. And Nathan Rawls considered his own were well in hand at the moment, at least so long as he managed to control his personal demon, which was his impatience with the day-to-day advance toward his goals. Days fled by; a man felt himself growing older, unfulfilled and obsessed with the sense of simply marking time. If he weren't careful, these resentments could get the better of him and lead him to foolish mistakes.

He picked up his pen, reversed the order of a couple of words he had written and struck out another. Yes, he'd done very well with the juicy story about Dallas Howbert and the poacher. It had been an unexpected plum — verification of everything he had been saying against the Cheyenne. It would make a fine box for the front page of this week's paper. Perhaps he should even consider putting out a four-page extra . . .

A glance at the silver turnip watch in his waistcoat pocket reminded Rawls of the hour, time for his regular mid-morning progress along Main Street — greeting friends and followers, buying someone a discreet drink of whiskey, picking up fortuitous bits of information, testing how the wind happened to blow from day to day. He rose, got his planter's hat off its hook and went out into a fine morning.

High above the roofs of town, white clouds scudded across the deep blue, shining in the sun; the warm wind was tanged by cookfires at the boomer camp. Rawls counted three new wagons there with approval. He made a note to meet the new arrivals later, bid them welcome, make himself known to them. Just for now he crossed the wide street to the Palace, knowing the ones he would be likely to find there.

And yes, there were the leaders of the boomer crowd — Pryor and Williamson and Stamper, the last looking bad with a black eye and his nose swollen and shapeless under a court plaster bandage, a reminder of the fight two evenings ago with the Indian. Stamper was still in a foul mood about that, cursing Johnny Logan and his employer, and the sheriff and anyone else he could blame.

There was much complaining about nothing being done to bring matters to a head, and an end to this intolerable waiting for action on the status of the reservation. Rawls, who saw a very real danger of these people wearying of hope too long deferred, took the occasion to tell them, "I think we're about due for good news, very shortly. In fact, I'm expecting a telegram." As he had known it would, this announcement caught the attention of the room and brought a flood of questions, but he simply shook his head and held up a palm to ward them off. "That's really all I can say now. You'll hear as soon as there's anything definite. You have my promise!"

He left them with that, knowing it would be enough to keep them talking — and his own name on their tongues — for the balance of the day.

Returning a half hour later to the *Advocate* office, he hesitated just a moment before entering, seeing that the

**89**

door behind the screen stood open. He was almost certain he had pulled it shut when he left. "Judge" Rawls scowled, briefly apprehensive. His right hand moved to the specially designed pocket of his waistcoat that held a tiny, two-shot Derringer. Then he yanked the screen wide, stepped quickly across the threshold and to one side, moving into shadow and out of the blast of noon sunlight framed by the opening.

He could detect nothing amiss; there was the smell of ink and paper, the familiar outlines of clumsy hand press and wooden boxes of type, filing cabinet and work tables. And then he made out the figure of a man, seated in a chair beside the desk, quietly watching him, the darkness of his skin blending with the gloom of the half-shadowed place. Rawls was startled, but he recovered quickly. "You!" he grunted. He hung his hat, walked back to the desk and stood staring down at Johnny Logan. "What's the idea, breaking in here like this?"

"A newspaper office is a place of public business, ain't it?" the Indian replied calmly. "The door wasn't locked. I didn't figure I was breaking in. I was just waiting to see you."

Rawls knew he had lost that point, so he merely grunted again. His eye lit on the sheet of foolscap lying prominently on the desk, the editorial he had been working on earlier. He indicated it. "I don't doubt you been reading this."

"I noticed my name," the other answered coolly. "Yes, I read it. I don't doubt I'll be reading it in your paper before long."

"Judge" Rawls tossed the editorial aside, hauled his barrel chair around to face his visitor and dropped into it. Logan met his stare as he demanded, "So what did you come here for?"

"To find out just how fair-minded a man you are," Johnny Logan told him without preliminary. "I always heard a newspaper was supposed to publish all sides of a question. I —"

"Maybe," Rawls interrupted scornfully, "you expect me to print some kind of denial that you helped that poacher escape the other day — in face of all the witnesses against you?"

The other shook his head. "It's not me I've come to talk about. It's the Cheyenne and what's happening on the reservation. You've been telling your readers that every Indian is a liar and a thief. But there's facts that might give a different picture if they were generally known, if you were to give them equal space."

Something in his manner turned Nate Rawls cautious. Eyes narrowing, he demanded, "Which 'facts', Logan?"

"That the Cheyenne are going hungry! That their rations are being cut off! By whom, or where, no one seems to know. And if some of them are stealing beef, it's because they're plain desperate!"

"I see . . ." *So he's been nosing into affairs on the reservation!* Rawls tried to conceal his alarm. He began to drum silently on the desktop with the tips of his fingers. "A touching story," he said, careful to put an edge of contempt into the words. "If one happens to believe it . . ."

"You can go over and take a look for yourself. Talk to Simpson, at the Walker Springs Agency. Question is, will you do anything of the sort?"

The two men looked at each other, and in that instant there was naked understanding between them. "I will do," Nate Rawls said bluntly, "whatever I damn well please!"

The Indian nodded his dark head. "That's what I thought. I'm well aware you've made up your mind to destroy the reservation. I guess you aren't apt to let anything interfere with that."

"Oh? You know, this is all very interesting," the other murmured, settling into his chair and hooking both thumbs into the pockets of his waistcoat. "Suppose," he suggested, "you tell me what else you know about me . . ."

"One thing I'd really *like* to know! With all the important connections you're supposed to have, could you just maybe have been aware — ahead of time, I mean — what was scheduled to happen to those rations? Were you *counting* on the Cheyenne going hungry, and maybe doing something desperate, when you set about launching your campaign against them?"

Rawls spoke quietly. "You really have an imagination, haven't you?"

"It doesn't take imagination to know a crook when I see one!" Johnny Logan said. He swung to his feet as though he could no longer bear to sit still and face this other man.

Nate Rawls remained as he was, fingers spread across the front of his waistcoat, head tilted slightly to one side, as he peered up at his visitor. He could feel the tightness of the muscles in his cheeks, hear the faint tremor in his voice that warned of the slackening grip on his temper. He said sharply, "You talk big for an Indian. Do you imagine anybody at all is going to listen to you?"

"Not to me, I guess," the other said, his black eyes boring into Rawls. "But they'll listen to Arne Jenson. You ain't fooled *him* any, you know. And when I've got through telling him about our talk, he's likely to have something to say. Mr. Jenson's one man people pay attention to . . ."

Suddenly "Judge" Rawls was on his feet. The two men locked stares for a long breath of time. Then, deliberately, Johnny Logan turned his back and started for the door. He had taken no more than a step when he heard the hiss of Rawls' in-drawn breath, and another sound that was not as easy to identify — like metal sliding over cloth. It was warning enough. He whirled in midstride to see the stingy gun with its large-bore twin barrels pointing at him, Nate Rawls's teeth bared by tight-drawn lips. Rawls promised, in a hoarse whisper, "No one's going to know what was said here!"

Looking into the deep-set, beady eyes, Johnny saw the determination to kill. It shook him but did not prevent him from moving fast. Only a step separated them. He took it at a stride, and his left arm came up, his reaching hand finding the other man's wrist and deflecting it, just as the ugly little gun spat flame. The crack of the weapon was startling. The ball spent itself

**93**

somewhere. Then Johnny's hand had closed on the gun, and the two of them were struggling for its possession.

Despite his cadaverous leanness, "Judge" Rawls had surprising strength. Locked desperately together, the two men trampled the splintered floorboards and fell, hard, against the edge of the desk. A blow of Rawls's bony fist struck Johnny's cheek, blindingly. Almost without thinking, Johnny hit back. He felt flesh give, and his knuckles stung with pain as they met protruding, rabbity teeth. Next moment Rawls had slid off the edge of the desk to the floor, leaving Johnny with the stingy gun.

Johnny had to catch his balance, and then he stood and simply glowered at the man huddled against the desk at his feet. Rawls was clearly dazed. The hair hung lank across his sweaty face, and there was blood on his mouth. But he gave Johnny a look of pure hatred, and something in Johnny turned cold as he met it.

Turning, Johnny flung the gun away. It struck the hand press with a metallic clang and went spinning somewhere. Afterwards, with the stink of burnt powder in his nostrils, he swung about and strode deliberately from the newspaper office.

A single gunshot, disturbing the quiet noon hour, would surely have caught attention. Emerging, Johnny saw a stir of movement on the porch of the Palace across the street. He thought he glimpsed the red beard of the man named Stamper. Knowing that he was being watched from over there, he tried not to show undue haste as he went around the hitch rack; but his hands

**94**

shook a little, jerking loose the knot in the reins, and his shoulders felt the weight of watching eyes as he lifted into the saddle of the black stud.

He heard the squeal of the print shop's screen door and looked around to see Nate Rawls come reeling out. Staggering, clutching at the edge of the door to steady himself, Rawls flung a pointing arm at Johnny and cried hoarsely, from a mouth smeared with dripping blood: "The filthy Indian tried to *kill* me! *Stop him!*"

Johnny swore, swung the black away from the rail and used the spur. The horse spurted forward, as yells broke out and boots trampled the steps of the saloon, men pouring down into the street. A gun opened fire, and then another. They missed, and men went rushing for their horses as they saw him escaping.

The shout of alarm was going up, all along the street. Within seconds the whole town seemed up in arms and bent on stopping the fugitive.

Just ahead of Johnny, now, a strange figure had appeared: an old man in a rusty black suit, thinning white hair standing in a halo about his head, the high sun reflecting smeared light from the metal badge pinned to his breast and from the long-barreled hog-leg revolver in his hand. It was the town's marshal, once a fierce and famous lawdog, now a frail and fragile man of eighty. He came stumping out into the street to face the rider on the galloping black, and he set himself there, raised his left arm and laid the barrel of the six-shooter across it, while he deliberately lined up his shot at the man hurtling straight toward him.

Johnny Logan shouted at him, his words lost in the pounding of hoofs and the hubbub of the street. And then the pistol blossomed with flame and a spurt of white smoke. He thought he felt the breath of the bullet singing past, only inches away. In the next stride, the black's shoulder struck and the old man was sent spinning aside. Johnny, plunging on, felt the breath catch in his throat and could only pray that he hadn't killed the marshal.

After that he was at the edge of town and away, the last houses falling back. But from the racket of the horses' hoofs behind him and the billowing dust, he knew the chase was only beginning.

# CHAPTER
# SEVEN

A vagrant whiff of tobacco, carried on the warm breeze, reached Bob Early as he eased down through a stand of aspen toward a spring where his horse could water. Power of suggestion lifted his hand toward the sack of makings in his shirt pocket, and he almost had it out when something struck him so forcibly that he pulled his animal to an uneasy halt.

*Who was smoking?*

He'd thought he was the only rider working this section of Bar J, not far from the reservation boundary, and certainly no one not on Jenson's payroll had any business here. Frowning, he shoved the tobacco sack back into his pocket and then stood in stirrups to search the thick mass of the aspen grove. The trees crowded the slope and this stock trail, a solid mass of busy, twinkling leaves that made the whole hillside appear to flow. The wind, blowing against his left cheek, told him the direction from which that telltale scent must have drifted. He tested for it, couldn't catch it a second time. From any evidence of sight or sound, he could be alone here on this whispering hillside, and the whiff of tobacco might almost have been his imagination — except that he knew it wasn't.

Bob Early shook his head. He touched the stock of the rifle in the scabbard under his right knee — he also had a six-shooter with him, but it was in a saddlepocket and not immediately handy — and then he sent the sorrel horse easing on down the stock trail. But as he rode, he was studying the shifting screen of leaf-shimmer, frowning and determined not to miss anything.

Abruptly the aspen gave way to alder, and as the slope flattened out, a level meadow opened in front of him. His head whipped around to a sound of something crashing through crowded brush. As he reined in, he glimpsed red hide, and then a steer came lumbering out into thick grass that was watered by the runneling and sun-sparkling spring. The animal trotted into the open and halted as it caught sight of Bob Early. It stood on spread legs, head lowered, peering and snorting uncertainly.

Where it had left the brush, a rifle shot lashed startlingly across the quiet. The steer simply folded onto its knees, rolled over in the long grass and died without a sound. Bob Early was left staring by the suddenness of it.

Belatedly he whipped his head around and saw the rider on the big blue roan horse at the edge of the alders. The branches partly hid him, but Bob Early thought he recognized the heavy outline of the man's shoulders. He saw the smoke trailing from the muzzle of the rifle in his hands and from the cigarette hanging from his mouth. Hot anger seized him. "Why, damn you!" Bob Early cried into the stillness that followed the rifle's report.

The rider turned his head, looked squarely at him, and the stock of the rifle came up to fill the hollow of his shoulder. Bob Early didn't think of retreating. He was pawing at the weapon in his own saddle boot. He slid it out, flipped it up and caught it in both hands, working the lever hastily to crank a cartridge into the chamber.

He had got that far when the other rifle spoke again. Bob Early felt the crushing blow that took him in the center of the chest. Pain exploded all through him, and then the blackness flooded in, and there was nothing any more.

It looked like touch-and-go for Johnny Logan. Since he broke out of town at a pelting run, with Nate Rawls crying his pursuers on, he had never once been able to lose the men who were after him. Some were plainly not horsemen, and probably none of them topped an animal that could hope to be a match for the black stud. Their numbers thinned as more and more were forced to drop out. But this left a knot of close to a dozen who would not be shaken, in spite of anything he seemed able to do.

A time or two he thought he had lost them, but when he drew up to let the black have a moment's breather, there was the swelling sound of galloping horses to warn him and make him urge the black on again. If they really thought he had tried to kill "Judge" Rawls, their champion, then he supposed he understood the

boomers' driving eagerness to have his hide —
especially when the leader was a red-bearded man with
a mashed nose and a pure need to settle for the beating
he took two nights ago.

Stamper saw his chance for revenge, and he for one
wouldn't give it up lightly.

A couple of times, when the pursuers thought they
had range, there was gunfire back there. After the first
gut-tingling reaction, Johnny Logan forced himself to
ignore it, aware that no one could shoot with any
accuracy from the back of a running horse. Soon he got
into timber and rougher country. As the river flats were
left behind, there was less chance for the men to use
their weapons.

Johnny toyed for a moment with the thought of
laying a trap, trying to get the lot of them under his rifle
and disarming them. But he rejected the plan as too
risky, and minutes later he was glad that he had.
Reaching the place where a tributary creek came
tumbling out of a rocky ravine, he impulsively turned
the black into the water. It broke in churning tumult
about them, as the stud strongly breasted the current.
Once it almost stumbled on the slick bottom, but a pull
at the rein, lifting its head, helped the animal catch its
footing. Next moment a curve in the creek bed brought
them in under an eroded bank. There was barely room
for a horse to stand, and the rider bent low over its
withers. Johnny pulled in here, spoke to the black to
calm it. The noise of water rushing around him,
amplified by the rocky overhang and drowning any
other sound, he could only wait with rifle ready,

watching the curve of the bank downstream for the first hint that his enemies hadn't been thrown off.

Minutes drew out. He never rightly knew how much time elapsed before he at last felt safe to leave his hiding place — straightening and stretching to ease cramped tightness from his bent shoulders, his clothing clammy and drenched by cold spray. Apparently all was clear. He let the rifle hammer down and slid the weapon back into the boot. Then he continued upstream, letting his horse take its time while he watched for a good place to climb out of the ravine . . .

He was late when he rode slowly in on the Bar J, being careful to keep off the skyline, in case Stamper and the others should be here ahead of him, watching. The sun was already setting, and shadows spread through the ranchyard. Lamplight was beginning to glow in various windows, while the blades of the windmill still bounced back a last smear of reddish light. Some fifty yards from the main house, Johnny dismounted in a patch of brush and tied the black, while he tested for any hint of danger.

Riders were coming in off the range and unsaddling at the barn corral. Men drifted through the yard or moved about the bunkhouse. Aromas of frying steak and boiling coffee came from the kitchen shack. It was a normal scene at the tail end of a working day. And now someone stepped from the door of the main house, to knock the dottle from a pipe and stand enjoying the evening as he scraped out the bowl with a knifeblade. It was Jenson, and Johnny Logan waited no longer. Even as his boss turned and walked back inside the building, Johnny left his place and started quickly across the yard.

It might have been the heart of an important ranch operation, but Arne Jenson's house gave no particular indication of it. He had added a couple of rooms to the chinked-log structure he had started with, but that was all. The fact that he was a bachelor could be guessed easily enough from its furnishings — the rough-hewn tables and chairs, the mounted head of a Dahl sheep on one wall, the bearskin on the floor, the rack containing a shotgun and a pair of rifles. The smell of the roughcut he used in his pipe permeated everything.

When Johnny opened the screen, his boss looked up from the stock paper he was reading. "Come in, come in," he said with his usual bluff informality. And then, as the younger man advanced into the lamplight, he read the look on Johnny's face, and his eyes narrowed. Jenson tossed the paper aside and rose to his feet. He said, "You look pretty wild, Johnny!"

Johnny could believe that. As he walked into the room, pulling off his sweat-stained hat, his attention was still mostly on the darkening night outside. He paused once to glance over a shoulder, before deciding that he had heard nothing untoward beyond the open door. He asked, "Has anybody been here looking for me?"

The rancher shook his head impatiently. "Ease off, boy! Take a chair, and tell me what's on your mind. How long since you've eaten?"

"That can wait." Johnny dropped his hat on a littered table and let himself slack into a chair, still too keyed up to relax. Arne Jenson, as though catching some of Johnny's anxiety, went to the door and made a long surveyal of the quiet ranchyard. Then he closed the door and put his shoulders against it, as he studied the younger man, not pressing him but letting him take his time.

Johnny ran a hand through his coarse black mane. "I got a lot to tell you," he said hoarsely. "So much, I don't quite know where to start."

"The beginning's usually a good place . . ."

"I guess that would be yesterday morning," he said. "It was my day off, so I rode over to the reservation. I —" Johnny hesitated. "I'm afraid I wasn't quite honest, Mr. Jenson, about that trouble I had with Dallas Howbert."

Jenson nodded. "You knew all the time who the Indian was he caught poaching? I guessed as much."

The younger man blinked. For a moment he floundered, unable to find words. "And yet — even so — you backed me with the sheriff?"

"I figured you had good reason for holding back his name. Or at any rate, I hoped so!" the rancher added in a tone that held an edge of iron.

Johnny swallowed; he forced himself to meet the rancher's stare. "I'm sorry, Mr. Jenson," he said doggedly. "I meant to play fair with you. But I felt I just couldn't say anything till I'd had a chance to talk to the man, myself, and try to find out what kind of story he had."

"I see." Jenson spoke shortly, and despite his explanation Johnny still felt that the other was disappointed in him. Stern of face, the rancher came back to the chair he had vacated. He dropped into it. "All right," he said gruffly. "Go on . . ."

"So I went over there yesterday, trying to find him," Johnny said. He proceeded to narrate his experiences at Lame Elk's village and at the Walker Springs Agency, and what he had learned there. He told it plain, without haste and without embellishment; but suddenly he broke off as he saw that his listener had lifted his chin from his chest and slowly turned to look at him.

At the scowl he read on the other's face, Johnny exclaimed harshly, "I'm not lying, Mr. Jenson! I swear! I got this on the word of the Indian agent himself and Mr. Cummings at the Indian school — two white men. Those people on the reservation are *hungry!* There's sickness among them, and in a few more months, when winter hits and they're still without food, and the supplies they need —"

A lifted palm interrupted him. "I'm not doubting your word, Johnny," the rancher said heavily. Rather, he sounded shocked and infinitely tired. "It just seems incredible," he went on, "something like this could be happening! The business of supplying the reservation is bound to be a complicated one. Maybe there's been a breakdown somewhere in communications . . ."

"Simpson don't think so," Johnny answered. "He thinks somebody higher up is stealing from the Cheyenne, and he ought to be one to know. Besides —" He hesitated. "I haven't told you everything."

Jenson's thick chest lifted on a sigh. "I'm still listening . . ."

There seemed no point in mentioning his brief run-in with Warren Brady's gunmen, and Johnny passed over that. "You weren't here last night," he said, "so I couldn't talk this over with you then. And there wasn't anyone in the bunkhouse I felt like discussing it with."

"I had to ride to Saunderstown on business," Jenson interrupted, in explanation. "I didn't get back till this afternoon."

"That's how I figured. Still, I had to do something with what I'd learned. This morning I was sent to check the wire on the hayfield north of Skull Creek. I got through before noon and so, on my own, I went on in to town. I wanted to talk to that newspaper fellow."

"Rawls?" Jenson's voice was sharp with puzzlement. "What about?"

"Two things," Johnny told him. "First, a hunch I had — that he'd known all along about the Cheyenne's trouble over their rations. Well he wouldn't come out and admit it, but I'm positive he was lying."

"And the other thing?"

"I challenged him to print that story in his paper. He laughed at me and ordered me out of his office." Johnny hesitated. "I guess, after that, I lost my temper. I told him I was going to report the matter to *you*, and that you'd have something to say about it. That was wrong, Mr. Jenson. I shouldn't have brought you into the thing, but I did, and I'm sorry. And then he pulled a gun on me!"

Arne Jenson received that in silence, waiting as Johnny finished telling of the fight in the office, Rawls's attempt to have him stopped, the pursuit from town. His story completed, Johnny Logan felt considerably let down and dry of throat from so much talking. He said solemnly, "The thing I hate worst is what happened to the marshal! I didn't mean to do that. I was trying to rattle the old man, break his aim before he was able to put a bullet in me. But I misjudged, and my horse struck him and knocked him down. In all the dust, I couldn't tell how bad I might have hurt him."

"Then I guess that's something we'll have to worry about later, ain't it?" Arne Jenson said shortly. "But the ones that chased you? Once you lost them, what was to prevent them coming here to the ranch and simply waiting to pick you off when you rode in?"

Johnny nodded solemnly. "I thought of that. It's why I was careful about showing myself and waited till dusk. But maybe they decided I wasn't worth the bother, after all."

Suddenly he found himself fighting a yawn. He lifted a hand and ran the palm downward across his cheeks. Out of weariness and fruitless worry, he forced himself to say, "Look, Mr. Jenson! Maybe it was kind of a stupid thing for anyone to do — riding into that town, and bracing Nate Rawls with all his friends in hailing distance. Especially when I really hadn't a damn thing to say to him." He shook his head. "But something's got to be done . . . and I don't know what! The Cheyenne —"

"You can't carry them all on your shoulders, Johnny," the rancher pointed out. "Though I guess I understand you wanting to try. They *are* your people

. . . But the problem ain't going to be solved tonight." He got to his feet, stood looking down at the younger man. "You had anything to eat?" he demanded.

Johnny shook his head tiredly. "Not since breakfast."

"You better get over to the kitchen, then, and get some grub in you."

"Yes sir." Johnny levered himself out of his chair, got his hat and started for the door. His boss halted him there, placing a hand on his shoulder.

"We'll talk more of this," he promised earnestly. "I've been trying to keep more or less out of things, as long as the Indians ain't touched any of my own beef. But what you learned at the reservation puts a whole new face on the matter. If they're deliberately being starved, then even Dallas Howbert should have to admit they ain't wholly to blame. And like you say, the *Advocate* should be made to tell the whole story, not just the part that Rawls and his land-grabbing boomers want to have heard. But for right now —"

And then he broke off, at Johnny's sudden exclamation: "Mr. Jenson, what do you suppose is going on out there . . ."

On a corral post, a lantern hung by its bail and laid streaky light across the deepening darkness. It showed a rider who had apparently just entered the yard, leading another horse that had an oddly shaped burden lashed to its saddle. Still mounted, he appeared to be the center of a clot of Bar J punchers. More were gathering at a run, dust stirring under their boots, excited voices swelling.

Johnny Logan said, "It looks like a body on that horse!"

He started forward but was checked by the tightening of the hand that lay on his shoulder. "I'll see what this is about," Jenson grunted. "You best stay out of sight, just in case your friends from town are out there somewhere watching for you!"

Johnny Logan nodded, but a premonition of dread gnawed at him as he stood back out of line of the door, watching Arne Jenson hurry in the direction of the barn.

The rider was Dick Stubbs. As their boss approached, the rest fell suddenly silent and dropped back, and Dick swung down from his horse. Jenson looked at the grim faces about him and demanded sharply, "Well?"

Stubbs indicated the motionless burden on the saddle of the led horse. "It's Bob Early," he said in a voice that had the iron of anger behind it. "He was murdered. One of them Injuns done it, boss!"

Jenson turned from a look at the body that was tied, belly down, across the saddle. "You *saw* this?"

"Didn't have to. I found his bronc, with the reins trailing. That animal never was broke proper, to stand. So I backtracked and found the kid, already getting stiff. He'd been shot in the chest — must have been dead for hours."

Dick Stubbs' voice began to shake with helpless fury. "It was murder, I tell you! And there was one of our steers, butchered — only the best meat taken, the rest left to rot. Plain enough, the kid come up while it was

**108**

going on and got shot for interfering. I found tracks of a single horse, going away — not wearing iron, and heading straight for the reservation. One of them Injun scrubs, not a doubt in the world, but it was coming on dark too fast to try and follow."

The story tumbled out of him, and then all of the men were waiting and grimly watching Arne Jenson, their eyes seeming to glitter in the streaky glow of the lantern. Bob Early had been popular with the crew. Jenson could feel their anger and detect its stirrings in himself. Still, as the one in charge, he couldn't allow himself the luxury of blind anger. Deliberately roughing his voice, he gave brusque orders: "Get him down from there. We'll have to put him in the barn until we can arrange decent burial."

For a moment the men continued to watch him in silence, plainly expecting something more. Jenson's mouth hardened. He rapped out a further order and at that, reluctantly, the group began to break up. But their mutterings told how far they were from being satisfied. It was Dick Stubbs who had the courage to demand, "And what about the one who killed Bob?"

Jenson returned his look with deliberate coldness. "What about him? You said, yourself, there was no hope of trailing the man tonight. By morning he can lose himself on the reservation, assuming that's where he went."

"Where else? That was an Injun pony — not a sign of a shoe iron. The Cheyenne ain't had any better friends on this range than the Bar J. Up to now they've left our beef alone, but I guess, at that, our turn was bound to come. With people like that, hardly a step away from savagery . . ." Arne Jenson turned away, leaving the other's bitter words unanswered; but his own thoughts were bleak enough as he gauged the temper of the angry crew.

On a sudden decision, he hailed one of the men and drew him aside. "Go to the kitchen," he ordered. "I want a couple of days' saddle rations. Meat, bread, coffee, and salt and flour — whatever the cook can put together in a hurry. Bring it over to the house."

The man nodded and hurried on his errand. Arne Jenson turned and strode to the bunk shack.

This was the crew's domain, and it was only rarely that the ranch owner invaded it. Jenson walked in now to find a somber atmosphere. Stunned by the death of Bob Early, the men seemed beyond talk. They sat about in silence, looking up wordlessly as their employer entered.

He said without preliminary, "Which one is Logan's bunk?"

With one accord the heads of the men lifted and turned to a bunk in the corner of the room. Jenson knew that there had always been considerable reserve between Johnny Logan and the other crew members, but he thought it was a distinct, if unspoken, hostility he could feel in them now. He walked back to have a look at Johnny's belongings. These were few enough — the blankets on the bed, a windbreaker and a shellbelt and gun hanging on a nail above it and, underneath, a canvas warbag containing extra clothing and such odds

**110**

and ends of possessions as a working cowpuncher was apt to accumulate.

In a continuing silence, Arne Jenson fell to work collecting these things. He rolled the blankets, took down the jacket and gun belt and made them into a single bundle. With his burden under one arm, he turned and stalked out of the building. He heard a muffled buzz of talk spring up in his wake.

As he reached the house, the puncher he had dispatched to the cookshack for supplies came hurrying with a gunnysack. Jenson ordered the supplies deposited on the wooden stoop beside the door. He placed the other things beside them and then went in to confront Johnny Logan.

For a moment the two men looked at one another. Then Johnny found his voice. "Sounded like I heard somebody out there say —" He swallowed an obstruction in his throat. "— say that Bob Early was dead! What happened, Mr. Jenson? Was there an accident?"

"No accident!" the other answered, biting off the words. He proceeded to tell Johnny news that made the young fellow's stomach turn over in sick horror. He tried to make some kind of answer but couldn't manage the words, and then he realized that Arne Jenson was looking at him with a peculiar searching stare. "You got any ideas about this?" Jenson demanded.

He frowned in bewilderment. "I ain't sure I know what you mean. You figure *I* can tell you who might have killed Bob?"

"They're your people. You know them better than anybody else."

Johnny drew a deep breath. "Mr. Jenson," he said, trying to hold his voice steady, "Bob Early was my friend. You can believe that if I was able to make any guess at all —"

"All right, Johnny," the older man cut him off. "I don't know what else I could expect you to say, and I do believe you. But a lot of things are changed now." Arne Jenson paused, frowning in the lampglow. He shrugged, drew a shapeless leather wallet from his hip pocket and took some greenbacks from it. "This should cover the pay you got coming," he said gruffly, "and a little extra. I've brought your stuff from the bunkhouse. There's a sack of grub on the porch. I think the sooner you leave here, the better."

Disbelieving what he heard, Johnny eyed the money in the other's hand. "You telling me — I'm fired?"

"For your own good." Jenson nodded grimly toward the thickening night beyond the door. "So far nobody's said anything, but I could feel the mood out there. Early was the best liked of any man in my crew."

"But they surely don't think —?"

"You're Cheyenne. Tonight, I have an idea nothing else really matters such a hell of a lot!"

So there it was. Johnny Logan had always known there were some who resented sharing space in the bunkhouse with a full-blooded Indian, but he had kept his distance from those few, had tried to do a good job and hold such friction to a minimum. He had actually let himself believe that he had been able to overcome most such prejudice in the time he'd been at Bar J. But he could see no good reason to doubt Jenson's word. Numbly he accepted the offered money and shoved it into a pocket of his jeans.

Jenson, though, wasn't quite finished. "If it was only the crew," he said, "I think I could probably keep them in line, though some, I'm afraid, would be bound to quit — men that I need. But there's more. There's a whole range to think about. God knows, it was bad enough before. A killing changes everything! You take my advice, you'll get out of this country — maybe clear out of Montana."

Johnny shook his head. "You're forgetting. You gave your pledge to the sheriff that I'd be here for trial in circuit court."

"I'll deal with the court."

"Mr. Jenson, I can't just run off and leave you to face that. And I can't run out on my people!"

But then he saw the rancher's mouth settle and harden, his face looking as though it might have been carved from stone. "Are you going to make me spell it out for you?" Arne Jenson demanded sternly. "I've tried to be fair with your people. I wouldn't have given a damn about the loss of a steer or two, if they're really starving. But, my God!" he cried hoarsely. "*Bob Early!*"

Something turned cold in Johnny Logan. He understood then what had happened. Whoever killed the Bar J puncher had cost the Cheyenne the tolerance and support and friendship of the one powerful friend they had had. With Arne Jenson turned against them, their last hope of an ally against the enemies who

**113**

wanted to strip them of their land was gone. Dazed and shocked as he was by the murder of his friend, Johnny knew that to have Arne Jenson turn against them could prove a real catastrophe for the Cheyenne.

A single glance at the Bar J owner was enough to tell that his mind was settled, and there was nothing to be gained by arguing. Besides, Johnny had no facts on which to base an argument. With a great emptiness inside him, he drew on his hat and walked out past the rancher. He found his belongings, and the sackful of food that Arne Jenson had been thoughtful enough to provide for him. He swung the burden to his shoulder and tramped off into the darkness, toward the brush where the black stud waited.

# CHAPTER
# EIGHT

In the shock of Bob Early's death and the hurt bitterness over his own firing, Johnny Logan had no intention of heeding any advice about leaving this country. He rode for an hour, while a white moon swam up the sky, and then found a cove of timber and boulders that looked like a place to camp. He staked out the black and made a circuit of his campsite, studying the land about in the revealing glow of moonlight. Satisfied that no enemy from town had followed him, or was likely to stumble across this spot, he returned to his horse, off-saddled, and broke out blankets and the grub Arne Jenson had provided.

It was a bleak enough camp, because he didn't feel like risking a fire. He ate his food cold, scarcely tasting it, still numb and brooding over everything that had happened. Later he made a final check on the security of his camp, moved the stud to another patch of grass and rolled up in his blankets; exhaustion claimed him.

By daybreak he was in the saddle again, casting for a sign.

Johnny didn't consider himself an expert on a cold trail, but, after all, any ranch hand was certain to pick up some amount of skill in following animal sign.

Moreover, he had a general knowledge of the area, close to the reservation boundary, where Early would have been working when he was killed. Dick Stubbs, hurrying to the ranch with his body, would have taken the most direct route. The trail shouldn't be too hard to find.

So Johnny was not really surprised when he rode down to a shallow ford, to let the black have a drink, and found quite by accident, there in the mud at the stream's edge, the sign he wanted. At any rate, that was his guess. Two horses had traveled this way, one ahead of the other, pointing in the direction of Bar J headquarters. The drying of the prints indicated that they could have been made sometime late the day before. It was good enough for Johnny Logan. When the black was ready, he splashed across the creek and began to backtrack.

It proved an easy trail to follow. Toward midmorning it led him over a hill crest and circled to skirt a stand of aspen and alders. On the slope below he found what he had been looking for.

Stony of face, Johnny Logan dismounted. The stud had caught the smell of blood, and it was acting up. He had to anchor the reins firmly to a stout aspen trunk, before he could move out for a look at what lay in the open clearing. Morning wind made a steady whisper in the tree heads, and there was a high, buzzing hum that swelled as he walked forward, to halt beside the remains of a slaughtered steer. Black flies hovered in a shifting cloud, briefly scattering as he nudged the carcass with a boot toe.

116

Johnny could see that only a few of the choicest cuts of meat had been taken, leaving all the rest. It was sheer waste, of a kind to tighten any cattleman's jaw in anger.

When he turned away from the cloying smell of death, he saw another smear of blood that must mark the place where Bob Early had been shot down.

The ground here was soft, turned almost to mud by seepage from a spring higher among the aspen. There were a good many tracks about, those of the slaughtered steer and those of the shod horses of Early and Dick Stubbs. He saw, too, the sharp prints made by high-heeled boots, where Stubbs had dismounted to hoist and tie the dead man on his saddle.

But there were more, and as he sorted them out Johnny Logan felt a cold knot form in his middle. Unmistakeably, he could make out the tracks of at least one unshod horse. And, where the butcher had knelt to do his cutting, there were impressions that could have been made only by someone wearing rawhide moccasins. Johnny shook his head. His expression was bleak as he turned away and allowed the swarming flies to settle again.

Mounted once more, he swung wide of that place of humming death and, picking up the trail of the unshod animal, set out after it. Only one horse, apparently — only one killer. He had wasted no time. With a murdered man behind him and stolen beef in his possession, he must have been in a kind of panic to get back to the protection of the reservation. He'd set his animal on the most direct line, and he'd kept a steady pace.

Since he knew now which way the tracks were leading, Johnny Logan did not need to keep a constant eye on them but pushed impatiently ahead, checking only at intervals to confirm his course. Once it took him onto a stretch of tough outcropping, where the tracks played out. Johnny did not let that stop him for long. He kept on confidently and was rewarded by picking up the sign just where he would have expected to.

But somewhat later, when he was almost in sight of the unmarked reservation boundary, it dawned on him that there was suddenly no trail at all to follow.

Reluctant to turn back and hunt for it, Johnny almost blindly pushed ahead. But in the next breath he realized the foolishness of that course and drew rein instead, swearing. The black appeared to sense his indecision and uneasily shook out its mane. Johnny spoke to reassure it. And then, deciding with a grimace that he really hadn't any choice, he reined about to look for the place where he had missed the cold trail.

When at last he located it, he understood how it could have happened. The killer had switched directions on him, turning aside without any warning into the head of a gully that opened to the north. The tracks were plain enough. If Johnny had been paying attention, he would have spotted them. Chagrined over the loss of time, and at letting himself be fooled by such a simple trick, he put the black into the gully, which deepened quickly, its walls rising on either hand as he descended.

**118**

From now on, he knew, he was going to have to be more alert. That rider evidently had more on his mind than simply beating the fastest possible retreat to the safety of the reservation.

Johnny Logan followed the trail into rougher country. The region ahead of him wasn't too familiar. Because of the lack of good grass or water, stock wasn't apt to stray in here, and none of the ranchers used it. A man trying to confuse pursuers, on the other hand, could find it made-to-order. Movement of the earth's crust had started erosion that resulted in a small badlands. Its heart was a long fault scarp, with a skirt of talus spread out at its foot, and Johnny knew the worst when he saw the sign of the unshod horse curving directly into this. He followed it there and sure enough, there he lost it.

Still he hung on doggedly, casting about and wasting valuable time, but finally had to call it quits. The litter of rubble and boulders, broken off the face of the scarp, wasn't going to show him anything whatever. Johnny Logan pulled up and sat a moment listening to the silence, and to a faint, fluting hum of wind in cracks of the cliff above him. Through the play of light waves on naked rock surfaces, he peered off with narrowed eyes toward the reservation somewhere ahead. He tried to work out the score.

Aloud he said, to no one at all: "No use kidding myself. It would take a pair of eyes better trained than mine to figure this one out!"

His voice sounded small against the stillness. The rim and the crumbled talus at its foot stretched away from where he sat, giving him back no answer. He could picture himself spending days poking around here and never again picking up the unshod pony's tracks. And with every passing moment the trail, already cold, was growing colder still. In complete frustration, he rubbed a hand down across his face, thinking of Bob Early lying murdered and the killer escaping.

And then his hand stilled, at a thought, something Howard Cummings had told him. Yes, that could be his answer! At least, he told himself as he took up the reins, it was probably the best chance he had. And that made it worth the trying . . .

Driven by impatience, he had been pushing hard all the way to Lame Elk's village, and the stud's black coat gleamed faintly with sweat. Johnny rode him at a walk into the circle of tepees and directly to the lodge of the man named Badger. The aroma of a cookfire and stew simmering in the pot reached him, and then the fire came into view and the young woman who knelt beside it. As his horse came to a halt, the girl lifted her head. It was Anne.

Still on her knees, she sank back and placed her hands upon her thighs and looked at him. He was struck once again, as he always was, with admiration for the shapely figure in the simple doeskin dress, the charm of huge black eyes in a heart-shaped face framed by glossy braids that hung down her breast.

Johnny glanced quickly about. The flap of the lodge entrance was closed. The boy he had seen the other time was just coming up from the creek, walking lopsidedly under the weight of a filled waterpail dragging at one arm.

"Hello, Anne," Johnny said. "Is Badger around? I need him."

She turned and spoke to the boy in the Cheyenne tongue, of which Johnny knew only a handful of words. The youngster gave him a stabbing look, and then put down his pail and went trotting off as if on an errand. Anne got to her feet now, and Johnny stepped down from the saddle, holding the reins as he faced the girl beside the fire. She told him, "I'm surprised to see you, Johnny. I had no idea."

"Me either," he said. "You're helping with Badger's family? How are they?"

"It looks hopeful anyway. I've been with them since Sunday evening. I brought food and medicine."

"Since Sunday," he repeated thoughtfully, and because one thing had to be certain, he added, "You should be able to tell me, then. Was Badger in the village yesterday afternoon?"

"Yes." Anne's brows drew down then, and she studied Johnny's face with troubled eyes. She placed a hand on his sleeve suddenly. "What is it, Johnny? There's something terribly wrong. With you I can always tell!"

He couldn't lie to her. "No use trying to hide it," he said gruffly. "To begin with, I've lost my job. Mr. Jenson fired me. For my own good, he said. He thinks I ought to leave this country."

Her ripe lips parted. "I don't understand!" she exclaimed, helplessly bewildered. He did not explain,

**121**

just then, for at that moment Badger appeared carrying a cheap-looking ax and an armload of chopped firewood. He must have got the message from his son, for he looked at Anne and Johnny with curious expectancy.

Johnny told him without preliminary, "Badger, I want you to ride with me."

"Ride where?" the other demanded.

"Yesterday someone killed a friend of mine and butchered one of my boss's steers, and then headed for the reservation. It's a cold trail, but Mr. Cummings said you have a reputation of being one of the best trackers among the Cheyenne. That's the kind of help I need."

The man's broad face was utterly without expression. Deliberately he turned to set down his armload of wood and get rid of the ax. As he did so, Anne exclaimed, "Johnny! Who was killed?"

"Young fellow named Bob Early," he told her. "You've heard me speak of him. I trailed his murderer as far as I was able, but I lost him. Looks to me, only a real expert could pick up his trail again."

Then Badger spoke, and his voice was heavy. "You think you make Badger follow this trail for you — to the reservation, to one of the people?"

"If that's where the trail leads," Johnny Logan answered. "Maybe it does, and maybe it doesn't. We don't know. Either way, I don't see I have a choice. Or you either," he added bluntly, holding Badger's eye with his own. "I saved your neck when you were in bad trouble. Now you owe me a favor, and I'm calling it in. Go get your horse."

122

He thought for a moment that the man was going to refuse. He hated using that kind of pressure, hitting Badger with his sense of obligation, but it wasn't a time for bargaining. Badger's look just then was completely savage, with unfathomed depths of black resentment behind it. Then the dark eyes seemed to turn opaque, and without a word he turned away, and Johnny Logan knew without any particular pleasure that he had won.

After that he had to look at Anne, for she was speaking in a voice that trembled. Her pretty face, when he looked at her, held disappointment such as he had never thought to see there. "Johnny, I can't believe it!" she cried. "If you find this man, what will you try to do? Kill him yourself? Take him in for the white man to hang? When you don't even know how badly he might have needed the beef he took!"

Johnny met the angry hurt in her eyes. Loving her as he did, he tried to remain gentle and reasonable in his answer. "And what about the man he killed?" he reminded her. "Bob Early was nearest to a good friend I had, among Mr. Jenson's crew."

For just a moment her look lost its steadiness. But high feeling pushed the words from her in a rush. "You don't *know* what happened. He might have *forced* the man to kill him. The white men won't care, or even bother to find out. They'll hang him out of hand!"

Her voice had turned a little shrill; her fists were clenched. Johnny, looking down at her face and her small, tense figure, was saddened to see her so upset and furious with him. He could only shake his head, a little helplessly, and tell her with grave simplicity: "Anne, I'm sorry."

And then Badger was there again, mounted on the same spotted pony that had carried him away from the fury of Dallas Howbert and his riders. Johnny wheeled and stepped up to the saddle of the black. Not looking at Anne, he kept his eyes straight ahead as he swung the stud around and motioned Badger up. Wooden-faced, the other man fell in beside him, and they rode away from there, leaving the girl standing beside the fire.

They had left the village and were climbing a rise beyond, when the drum of a running horse sounded at their backs. Johnny Logan looked around, and when he saw the rider making toward them, he gave an exclamation under his breath but pulled in, the black turning under him in a nervous circle. Badger, seeing him halt, also stopped to wait, a stoical lack of expression on his broad face.

Anne was an expert horsewoman. She rode effortlessly and with grace, strong brown legs gripping the saddleless barrel of her pony, slim body easily erect. She came on to within a yard of Johnny before she eased her animal to a halt. To judge from the way she met Johnny's look, her jaw set in defiance, she plainly expected trouble and was ready.

Before Johnny could speak, Badger rapped out in Cheyenne what seemed to be an anxious question. The girl answered, then looked coolly at Johnny as she translated for him. "Jane Hummingbird said she'd be willing to sit with Badger's woman for a little while. I'm going with you. And don't say I can't!"

124

He would have forbidden it, but he held his tongue. It was sad to see the rift that had suddenly opened between them, a rift caused by this new and unfamiliar distrust. It was as though she looked at him across the gulf of race, forgetting her own good treatment by the Cummingses, seeing in Johnny someone who would betray his own kind to the white man. He had been called a "white Indian" before, and it had angered and hurt, but nothing as bad as this.

Johnny Logan's mouth tightened. He didn't trust himself to speak. He showed his displeasure in the way he turned from her, and, without a word or another look in Anne's direction, booted the stud ahead.

He couldn't take out his frustrations by punishing the black; nonetheless, he set a stiff pace. Even so, his companions had no difficulty keeping up. Anne was a natural horsewoman, as Johnny well knew, and he'd seen the way Badger set his pony in pellmell, reckless flight, making his escape from Howbert's men. Rather sooner than expected, the line of the fault rim began to cut the sky ahead; the cliff's face seemed almost to swell and soar as they neared. Presently Johnny Logan pulled up and pointed to the jumble of scattered talus.

"There you are," he told Badger gruffly. "He rode into that stuff, and I count at least a dozen erosion gullies he could have followed, leaving it. I'd need at least a week to try and check them all for tracks."

Badger made no answer. They rode into the boulder field, the cliff rising directly above them now, to meet a sky of such dazzling blue that, looking at it, one's vision seemed to swim with points of light. A hawk took off from a nest under the rim and swept silently away until the sky swallowed him. A faint humming of wind made its organ tone in those steep vertical cracks etched in the wall's surface.

Badger had been studying the rubbled ground. He said suddenly, "Maybe he don't come this way."

"What else?" Johnny demanded. Instead of answering, the other tilted his head to peer at the cliff, eyes narrowed against the fierce light reflected off it. Johnny saw, and exclaimed, "You don't mean, up *over* the rim? I thought of that myself, but no man could ride a horse up one of those breaks. He'd never be able to hang onto its back!"

"Don't have to *ride!*"

It took a moment for Johnny Logan to get his meaning. Then it struck him. "I see! You're saying, if he was at all surefooted — especially, if he happened to be wearing moccasins — a man might be able to climb up there and *lead* his animal. Likely, at that, it's not really as steep as it appears to us from here."

"Maybe," Badger said again, with a shrug to tell Johnny that he could take the idea or not, as it pleased him.

It pleased him considerably. Thrusting his boots into the stirrups, he lifted the reins as he said briskly, "We'll have a look. It can't take much more time than has already been wasted. And I got a hunch . . ."

In order to flank the fault line and locate a route to get up on top, it was necessary to swing south for almost a mile. Badger was the one who found a game trail, making an easy climb of it. He led the way, and on

**126**

cresting the rim, they were given a far view of the miles stretching off below them, toward the reservation. North and west, a dark line of timber broke the rolling flow of land.

A warm wind blew strongly here; it caught Johnny's hatbrim, flattened it back against his head. He flipped it down into place again and looked at Badger, nodding to indicate that the job was in his hands. Without a word the Indian started away, watching the ground. Johnny glanced at Anne and caught an odd expression in the eyes that studied his face. She seemed less hostile toward him than before, more thoughtful now.

He didn't try to speak to her. He nudged the black, following Badger's spotted pony along the rim. Presently he heard the girl coming after him.

In the end, the sign proved remarkably easy to locate. Suddenly Badger had halted and was turning to signal, and at once Johnny Logan spurred to join him. A tingle of excitement swelled as he drew rein and took a look for himself. The man had climbed a slant that might have given him little trouble at first, but it steepened near the top, and the last yards must have been a scramble, to judge from deep gouges where the unshod horse had dug at the crumbling surface for footing.

They had made it, though probably at the expense of a badly frightened horse. Once on top, Johnny could see where the animal had danced around, almost as though in a panic, before it could be brought under control. And among the hoofmarks there was one distinct, deep print of a round-toed moccasin, made probably as the man launched his weight once more onto the horse's back.

Badger pointed, without speaking, toward the line of timber to the west. Johnny nodded and again let the other man take the lead.

When they rode under the trees, he couldn't make out much in the carpet of bark and needles. But even here, Badger seemed to be put off hardly at all. He rode straight through, and Johnny and the girl followed him out of the shadow of the pines. Moments later they dropped into a deeply silted dry wash. It was sheltered from the constant wind, and even after the passage of hours the tracks were clearly visible, their edges sharp. It was there that Badger waited to let Johnny catch up.

"Left front hoof," he said briefly. "Split bad."

Now that it was pointed out to him, Johnny saw it at once — an unmistakable notch in the toe, leaving a mark almost as distinct as the split hoof of a deer. He speculated that it could have been damaged during the wild scramble over broken rock. Thoughtfully he considered the tracks that climbed the farther, shallow bank of the wash and on to the rolling dips of dry grassland beyond. He drew a slow breath.

"I guess you see what this means? Wherever he's headed, it's not the reservation. That's no Indian we've been trailing. The sign he left was just supposed to make us think so."

Badger and the girl were staring at him. It was the latter who demanded to know, "Are you saying that some white man deliberately pinned murder on the Indians?"

128

"No, I think that killing was an accident." Patiently he explained. "It's my feeling, Bob Early stumbled onto a steer being butchered and had to be put out of the way. But if the idea was to turn Bar J against the Cheyenne, it could hardly have been planned any better. Not after they saw the evidence — those moccasin prints and what looked like tracks of an Indian pony." Johnny's face was grim as he indicated the plain marks in the creek bed.

Then, to Badger, he added, "Many thanks for your help. From here on, looks like the trail shouldn't give any problems."

Badger said, with heavy skepticism, "Maybe."

"I say no," Johnny answered firmly. "I can manage. And the way feelings are, it could go damned hard right now with any reservation Indian found where he doesn't belong. I want you home with your family. I mean it!"

He knew the reminder of his ailing family would weigh heavy on Badger. The man thought about it, his broad features showing little. A lift of his shoulders, then, in an expressive gesture, and abruptly he jerked his pony around with the rope he used for reins. He buckjumped up the shallow bank of the draw and cantered back the way they had come, quickly disappearing into the trees.

Johnny turned to the girl. He said quietly, "That goes for you too, Anne."

She didn't seem to hear. She was looking at him oddly, and now she blurted, "You knew all along, didn't

**129**

you? You knew it wasn't an Indian. But why did you let me think — ?"

"I *didn't* know," he interrupted, his voice hard. "I was only hoping. And I had to mean just what I said. I wanted the one who killed Bob Early. It couldn't matter whether he was a white man or a Cheyenne."

For a moment neither spoke. "I guess I understand," the girl said at last. "I didn't before, and I'm sorry. I should have known I wasn't being fair to you — and only making a bad time worse. I —" Her voice broke off, and Johnny saw her wide eyes glisten suddenly with tears.

He reached over and touched her hand. "I know how it must have looked," he told her gently. Abruptly he drew away, and his tone changed. "Right now, I want you to go back."

"While you follow blindly after that killer?" she exclaimed. "And risk getting killed, yourself?"

"I promise I won't push my chances. Does that satisfy you?"

Anne looked at him directly. "No!" she exclaimed in a muffled voice. But she pulled her pony around and kicked it with moccasined heels.

Johnny watched her small, erect figure, fitting itself so trimly to the movement of the horse. He almost called something after her, then shook his head. Instead, he spoke to the black and sent it on along the plain line of tracks. At a little distance, he turned and looked back once.

The girl had halted her pony and was sitting motionless, watching him. Johnny lifted a hand, wasn't sure that she could see the gesture. A moment later he dropped into a swale and left her out of sight, behind him.

# CHAPTER
# NINE

There was blood, and there were chewed and splintered bones with shreds of the meat still clinging to them, and some tattered remains of burlap sacking. Johnny Logan didn't have to get down for a closer look to know what had happened here. The sack and its contents had been tossed carelessly into the brush, where some night animal had found and dragged them out and, after a meal, had left the scattered evidence for anyone to see.

The black didn't like it and snorted uneasily to rid its nostrils of the hated blood smell, but Johnny, tight-lipped, held a close rein. Bad enough to kill and butcher another man's beef. It was the final outrage to throw away the choice meat for any scavenger to find.

Pressing on, Johnny maintained the pace he had been holding to, scarcely needing to halt now or even slow briefly to take his bearings. During the past hour, with every mile he had grown surer there was only one place where the tracks could be taking him. At first he hadn't believed it. Now he did, and his anger steadily deepened.

A smear of sunlight on white paint and new roof shingles alerted him, and he pulled aside toward a

132

stand of pine that would cover his approach. When he had worked through that, he dismounted and had a careful look.

He had been here before, having ridden over once with Arne Jenson on ranch business. There was considerable contrast between this place and Jenson's. For all its size and importance, Bar J's headquarters buildings were log-constructed and weather-beaten. It would have been hard to tell the owner's house from the bunkshack. But here sawn lumber had been hauled in, and an array of well-constructed, white-painted buildings was set off by the battery of corrals and barns and the lesser structures of a working outfit. The main house set apart, surrounded by a neat picket fence, a tall and narrow two-story building with eaves dripping elaborate scrollwork. From an arch above the gate hung a slab of wood with the B Cross design burnt into it.

The whole layout seemed a tribute to the vanity of Warren Brady, a small man whose possessions had to make up for his unimpressive stature.

Johnny Logan stood beside his horse under the trees and studied the place during long minutes. Everything was surprisingly still for a working ranch. He saw no one moving about the buildings, and of the three big corrals, only one held a couple of horses at the moment. Of course, this was the busy season, and normally you wouldn't expect to see many of the crew around headquarters at the middle of the day. But B Cross was no normal outfit. Johnny Logan wasn't forgetting Clayt Gannon and his chosen cronies. Whatever their positions here, those men certainly hadn't been hired to do an ordinary cowhand's work for day wages.

Exactly what it was they *had* been hired for, Johnny was beginning to have some suspicions.

Yet it didn't look as though any of that bunch was around, either. In the bunkshack perhaps, but though he watched it carefully, while time dragged away, he could see no sign of life there. He found his attention returning to the pair of horses in the corral.

One was a brown, the other a blue roan. That either of these, of all the riding stock to be found on a ranch this size, might turn out to be the one he was interested in seemed rather unlikely. But as he watched them moving about in the pen, Johnny knew perfectly well that he meant to check them out. With his eye he measured the distance between him and the corral, noting the lay of the land and a row of sheds that should offer a shield from view of the main buildings. He made up his mind.

A quick knot in the reins anchored the black to a pine bole; a final glance at the blank windows of the main house standing elegantly among the lesser buildings, and he started forward. He moved lightly, keeping low and using any cover of bush or declivity until he reached the sheds, where he paused to settle his breathing and test again for danger. He had spotted one building, with a stovepipe chimney and a row of garbage tins on a rack beside the door, that he took to be the domain of the ranch cook. No sound from there, no trace of smoke lifting from the chimney.

That struck him as rather odd . . . He ghosted forward again, circling the corrals and bringing up beside the one that held the horses.

The brown horse caught his scent, loosed a snorting whinny and quickly whirled away toward the farther side of the corral. As it did so, Johnny caught the glint of sun striking shoe iron. He filed the brown away for future consideration and turned to the roan. It stood unmoving, looking at him and waggling its ears — apparently of a more phlegmatic temper, not so ready to react in alarm to sight or smell of a stranger. Johnny slipped one leg between the bars and slid through in a single unhurried movement. Standing inside the pen, he spoke quietly to the roan, which moved its head a little and stamped a hoof into the mud but held its position. Talking quietly to reassure it, Johnny went closer. The horse looked at him but gave no sign of bolting.

He laid a hand on the animal's neck, felt the hide twitch. When the animal made no other move, he went carefully to a crouch and took hold of its left front leg. Without any resistance, the roan let him raise the hoof for a quick inspection.

It took no more than a glance. There were the clear marks where the shoe had been pulled — and in the toe, the deep split that matched the prints he had followed here. Johnny felt his breathing go shallow. Making certain, he proceeded to check the animal's other hoofs, the docile roan standing and letting him move around it and lift each of its legs in turn. There was no doubt left. All four irons had been deliberately pulled. It could only have been by design, not by any accident.

Johnny Logan straightened, a hand resting on the roan's shoulder, as he thought about the meaning of this. A voice spoke behind him. "Find something interesting?"

He froze. Carefully, then, he turned his head and saw the man looking through the bars at him, both forearms resting casually on one of them, a six-shooter indifferently but efficiently pointed at Johnny Logan's chest. The face above the gun was one he didn't recognize — dark-browed, loose of mouth, the lantern jaw pocked as though with the scars of an old disease. Johnny had an instinctive feeling that this wouldn't be one of Warren Brady's regular crew.

The man was studying him with narrow interest, and now he nodded to himself. "I'll be damned!" he grunted. "You must be that Indian of Jenson's. Guess I shouldn't be surprised, after what I been hearing about you." His voice hardened. "Just what did you think you were up to?"

"Making sure of something," Johnny told him bluntly, not letting him see any fear of the gun. "And I guess I have!"

"You've stuck your nose into trouble, is what you've done," the other said harshly. The gun in his hand was rock steady, now firmly trained on the Indian. "Keep those hands where I can see them!" he ordered. "And walk over here! Slow!"

There was no way to quarrel with that naked gun. Johnny did as he was told, careful not to let any dismay

**136**

show on his dark features. At a word from his captor, he moved so that his hip holster was placed within reach, and the man put an arm through the bars, plucked Johnny's six-shooter from the leather and tossed it aside. After that he stood ready, while Johnny Logan slid out between the poles. His captor nodded toward the bunkhouse. "Over there . . ."

There was nothing else for it. That gun meant business, and Johnny Logan saw no choice but to obey orders. He listened to the sound of those other boots behind him, keeping pace with his own as he approached the low, shake-roofed building where the B Cross crew had their quarters. Once again the stillness struck him, particularly the lack of any activity at the kitchen shack. It was unusual, in his experience, for the ranch cook not to be at his post, baking bread or pies or in some other way keeping busy during the long hours of afternoon.

The bunkhouse door stood open. As Johnny stepped across the wooden slab that served as a doorstep, he saw that a poker game of sorts was in progress. One of the players, in jeans and red underwear tops, was wrinkled and completely bald. Johnny saw the dishtowel apron tucked up around his waist and then understood about the silent cookshack.

The man who sat facing the door was the ugly one named Mitch, whom he'd encountered on the trail with Clayt Gannon a couple of days ago. He looked up as shadows filled the doorway, and his hands froze in the act of shuffling the greasy deck of cards.

"Look what I found down at the corral," he who held the gun said, past the prisoner's shoulder. "He was messing around that old blue roan horse of yours, Mitch."

"Like hell he was!"

"It's a fact! Looking at his hoofs."

For a moment no one spoke. The bald cook was peering from man to man, head turning as though his long neck were a swivel. Johnny and Mitch remained perfectly motionless, their stares locked. Johnny, aware that he was looking at Bob Early's murderer, could almost read the busy speculations furiously at work behind the other's pale eyes.

Mitch stirred slightly, put down the deck and motioned to an empty place across from him. At once Johnny received a shove from the man with the gun and let himself be forced into the chair, where he stared at Mitch across the scatter of poker chips. He could feel the threatening presence of that naked weapon close behind him.

Common sense told him he should keep his mouth shut and make the others do the talking, but bitter anger made him reckless. In any event, Mitch must know that his presence here, and his interest in the hoofs of the roan in the corral, could mean but one thing. He let the words pour out, almost of their own volition: "Wasn't as easy as you thought to bury a trail. You left clear sign, all the way from the place where you killed Bob Early."

If he thought the big fellow would attempt to deny the charge, he was wrong. "That was the fellow's name, was it?" Mitch countered, acknowledging his guilt without a qualm. He shrugged. "His own damn fault he got hurt. He busted in on me just at the wrong time."

"And for that, you killed him?" Johnny tried to hold his hands still where they lay, on the edge of the table. The big man's easy admission made it almost impossible to sit here and return his mocking look.

"Well, it wasn't personal," the other assured him easily. Then his face got hard and he added, "But *you*, now. You've turned out a nosy sort of bastard, ain't you? What else have you been up to?"

"I found where you threw away the meat from my boss's steer that you butchered."

The pale eyes skewered him. "You did?" the big man prompted softly.

Suddenly a hand fell on Johnny's shoulder and jerked him around to face the man who had captured him. "Damn you, who did you bring here with you?" The gun lifted, pointing at his head. "How many more are out there, Injun? You better talk!"

"Oh, hell, Chet!" Mitch chided him, as Johnny's mouth clamped shut. "There ain't any more out there. This boy is the kind that works alone. And a sneaky, red-skinned sonofabitch he is, too. Of course, you're welcome to go out and scout around. But I think you'll find I'm right. He's all by himself."

"I dunno what makes you so sure." But Chet Durkin, though scowling and plainly uneasy, relinquished his painful grip on Johnny Logan's shoulder. He did not volunteer to follow Mitch's suggestion and go prowling the yard to look for other intruders.

"I just don't understand," Johnny Logan said bluntly, facing Mitch across the table. "You men draw your pay from Warren Brady, and yet here you are playing "Judge" Rawls's game for him — even faking evidence that's sure to help him and his boomers against the Cheyenne! But Brady and Rawls aren't even on speaking terms . . ." Then, as he saw something begin to take shape in those mocking, pale eyes, a startling thought struck him. "Or — could it be that's what they *want* people to think?"

At this, the other's lips split in an open, mocking grin. "Well, now!" Mitch grunted, and he cast a look first at the silent cook and then at Durkin, looming behind Johnny's chair. "Ain't he the smart young Injun, though?"

"Look!" exclaimed Durkin, real uneasiness in his voice. "I honest-to-God think this is a matter for Brady to deal with. Him and Gannon was supposed to have ridden over to the Clevenger place this morning. Maybe one of us better go and —"

"No!" Mitch cut him off harshly. "Brady will have plenty of chances to do whatever he wants with him. *I* ain't through yet. I kind of want to find out what other smart guesses this smart Injun has been making."

Johnny Logan said, "Then what I said was right? Brady and Rawls are actually working together?"

"Hell, yes! They just been putting on an act for those dumb boomers. At first, they figured them reservation bucks would get hungry and start killing beef and stir things up; but that didn't happen fast enough. So then

**140**

Brady hired us to come in and help things along by doing a little poaching of our own."

Johnny shook his head, really perplexed. "I don't understand. Why should Brady, a *rancher*, want to cause trouble that can only end by overrunning this country with homesteaders?"

"Why, as for that," the big man said with a shrug, as he picked up the deck again and idly began shuffling it, "Rawls has an idea he sold the boss a bill of goods. He keeps talking about the benefits for Grady, having someone he can trust holding down an important job in Washington . . ."

Behind Johnny's chair, Chet Durkin shuffled his boots and began an anxious protest: "Mitch!" But the latter paid him no heed.

"What Rawls don't know," Mitch went on grinning at Johnny while his hands fiddled with the greasy cards, "is if and when the reservation *does* go up for grabs, Warren Brady don't intend to stand by and let any bunch of nesters divide it up."

"They want it awful bad," Johnny pointed out. "They'll fight, and some of them are pretty tough."

"Some of those landrushers in the Cherokee Strip run, last fall, thought *they* was tough too, but you ought to seen what Clayt Gannon and us done to them!" Johnny must have shown his lack of comprehension, because the man went on to explain, grinning hugely: "Sure thing! The bunch of us was hired, at good wages by people that knew ahead of time just which claims they wanted. The night after the big run, we had the job

**141**

of riding around through the Strip and cleaning them off.

"No fuss, no trouble to speak of — just a little plain language and a look at our guns! That was usually all it took to persuade those pilgrims they wanted to be somewhere else right then. I think only one or two insisted on getting shot." He chuckled at the memory, thick shoulders lifting. "A right smart number of claims changed hands because of us, all in that one night."

"And you're telling me the real reason you're in this country, is to repeat for Warren Brady the job you did in the Cherokee Strip?"

"We work for any man that pays our price," Mitch assured him. "If Rawls and his boomers can get the reservation thrown open, we'll make sure that Brady ends up owning all the best parts of it . . ."

Durkin had had enough. While Johnny sat stunned, absorbing what he'd learned, Durkin stepped in to slap a palm down hard upon the table top. "Damn it, Mitch! You don't have to tell everything you know!"

"He ain't going to repeat any of it," Mitch replied easily.

"That's what *you* say! All the same, I'm going after Brady and Clayt. Right now!"

"The hell you are!" Mitch lunged up out of his chair, sending it toppling. He looked even bigger on his feet than Johnny Logan had remembered him looking on his horse. "You'll go when I say to," he told Durkin, almost shouting. "Brady will have his turn. This is mine!" And he started around the table.

142

Durkin's reply seemed to die in his throat. Johnny Logan eased to his feet, cautiously watching the big man come at him. "This is the dirty Injun thinks he can lick a white man," Mitch declared. He gave the empty chair a boot, out of his path. And then his thick right arm was swinging.

Johnny tried to fall away from it, but the hard fist caught him on the side of the head, and he went down. Through the ringing in his head, he heard Mitch saying, "That's for dumping me off my saddle. Now get on your feet, and we'll see just how tough you are."

The baldheaded cook, who had yet to put a word in, was scrambling up from the table; Durkin had backed clear. Johnny Logan found himself alone, with the threatening Mitch rearing over him. He looked up at the fists, clubbed and waiting. He didn't think he stood much show against them; but if he didn't get up from there, his chances would be even less against those scuffed cowhide boots. Something told him that there would be no interference from either Durkin or the cook. Nobody was going to save him from what lay ahead.

Shaking his head, as though to clear it, he put his hands against the splintered floorboards. He pushed up to his knees and from there, staggering a little, to his feet. It might give him some slight edge, he thought, if Mitch could be made to think that first blow had him hurting worse than was actually the case. It had hurt bad enough: it had taught him solid respect for the power behind those thick-knuckled fists.

He had scarcely got his feet set when Mitch came after him again. Moving faster than the man likely thought he could, Johnny managed to duck under the blow aimed at his head and to use both of his own fists. He hit the big man in the chest and, when that stopped him briefly, was able to sink another blow in, just above the belt buckle. That one, at least, caught Mitch by surprise, and some of the wind came out of him in a startled grunt.

But he was less hurt than stung to fury. He recovered quickly and charged in, throwing wide haymakers. Johnny was unable to get out of the way and took a hard clout on the left cheek, followed instantly by the iron-sweet tang of warm blood. He was driven back, thrown off balance.

The natural instinct would have been to continue retreating; but the knowledge that this was the man who had killed Bob Early pumped a heady anger through him, and the pain of Mitch's blows only turned him reckless. Schoolyard bouts with older kids, who sneered at him for being Indian, had given Johnny plenty of training at fighting bigger opponents. He stood his ground, and his next swing caught Mitch hard, near the hinge of his massive jaw.

The big man went staggering. The table got in his way and collapsed under him, a pulled nail screeching as cards and poker chips flew. Mitch rolled down the slant of the table top and hit the floor, where he floundered bellowing.

Panting and waiting, fists ready, Johnny Logan heard movement just behind him. He had ignored Chet

Durkin, thinking this was to be a fight between him and Mitch alone. Too late, he started to turn and saw the barrel of a revolver striking at his head. He ducked wildly. The hat, which somehow had not been dislodged in the fight, cushioned the swiping blow and took off some of its edge. Even so, pain blossomed inside Johnny's skull, and he had to clutch at the back of a chair while the room reeled about him. He stood and fought the weakness in his own knees, waiting for another blow of the gun barrel to finish him.

It never came. Instead, Mitch was there again, back on his feet, face bloody and twisted with rage at the man who had downed him, even if only for a moment. Johnny had little more than a blurred glimpse of the glaring eyes and savage mouth. Then Mitch struck, and Johnny took the full weight of the bludgeoning fist. Stars exploded, and he was catapulted across the room. He struck against something hard and crumpled to the floor, as the lights flickered and went out.

# CHAPTER
# TEN

It was the edge of one of the bunks that Johnny had struck when he hit the floor. He lay half-propped against it, head ringing and the world seeming to pulsate darkly in ragged time with his own heartbeat. The buzzing in his skull gradually cleared, to become voices somewhere directly in front of him. As he picked up the thread of their talk, he knew he could not have been unconscious more than a moment or two, if he had actually blacked out at all.

Chet Durkin's voice, in the middle of a sentence: "— what Clayt Gannon or Brady will have to say about this."

"They got nothing to say," Mitch retorted. "It's *my* trail he followed here. I'm the one that swings if he gets anybody to listen to his story. I ain't taking any chances."

Vision settling, Johnny now was able to make out the pair standing over him. There was the dull gleam of gun metal in Mitch's hand, the barrel slanted down, the muzzle gaping blackly. He could see the heads of the bullets in the revolver's cylinder, and all at once he knew that Mitch was about to kill him.

Durkin caught the big man's arm, exclaiming, "For God sake, don't plaster him all over the damn bunkhouse! Haul him outside first. We have to *live* here!"

The big man hesitated, scowling fiercely. His face showed clearly the mark of Johnny Logan's fist. But he shrugged then and lowered the gun, and he said roughly, "All right. Grab his other leg . . ."

Something was screaming silently inside Johnny, telling him he had to stir himself, to make some effort, or it would all very quickly be over. Yet a strange lethargy gripped him, born of the battering he'd taken from Durkin's gunbarrel. Johnny felt incapable of movement, even when Mitch leaned and seized him by a boot. The Indian tried to speak, felt his throat swell to the effort but heard no sound come out.

Chet Durkin, also reaching to lay hold of the prisoner, straightened suddenly, and his head jerked on his shoulders. "What the hell was that?" he grunted. And then: "Hey! Something's after the horses!"

It came again — a frenzied, terrified squealing from the direction of the corral. Durkin let out an oath and started for the door, already running. He left Mitch with the prisoner. The commotion at the pen continued, and the big man also appeared to take alarm. As he turned away to follow Durkin he tossed an order at the cook, standing confused amid the litter of chips and cards and broken table left by the fight. "Keep an eye on him," Mitch said, indicating Johnny Logan. After that he, too, was gone.

Left behind, the prisoner and the baldheaded man regarded one another. The cook appeared to be unarmed. At least, there was no weapon bulge beneath the dish-towel apron tucked around his waist. He had taken no part in these happenings, had seemed in fact a more-or-less reluctant witness. It occurred to Johnny Logan that it might be possible to take him, that chance might have handed him a last opportunity to save himself.

He told himself, *Get up from there!* but his fuddled brain still refused to obey his will or do anything to make his body work. Perhaps the cook sensed this. The man kept swiveling his head, to look first at Johnny and then over at the doorway, as though torn between the command that had been given him and his natural curiosity to see what was happening outside. At the corral, the horses were keeping up their racket — shrill trumpetings of pure terror and, once, the splitting sound of a shod hoof striking against a pole.

Suddenly there was a gunshot — then another. That was more than the baldheaded cook could resist. He was outside the doorway at once. He lifted a shading arm and peered in the direction of the horse pens. Whatever had caused the disturbance there, the trouble now seemed to be subsiding.

Something thudded onto the blankets, close to Johnny's ear, where he sprawled against the bunk. At first the muffled sound scarcely registered. When it did, he twisted about with an effort and found himself staring at the gleaming tube of a rifle practically

**148**

touching his cheek. For a moment he could do no more than look at it, wondering how it had got there.

A voice spoke his name in an urgent whisper. "Johnny! Are you all right? Can you hear me?"

He managed to raise his eyes and, incredulous, saw Anne's face framed in the open window above the bunk. When he didn't answer, she spoke louder, trying to penetrate his dazed confusion. "Johnny, they're coming back! Pick up the rifle. Please!"

At that moment he heard the tramp of boots and the murmur of voices approaching. That spurred him out of his lethargy. He found the strength to raise an arm, take hold of the rifle and drag it off the bunk into his lap. By feel more than by sight, he recognized the weapon as his own saddle gun. Huddled there with his back against the bunk frame, he got the rifle into position. It seemed to take a great effort simply to work the lever and jack a shell into the chamber.

Outside, Chet Durkin was answering the cook's stammered question. "Rattler got into the corral and scared the horses. Mitch knocked its head off." And now Mitch tramped inside, his boots shaking the floor, the gun he had used on the snake still gripped in his fist. He was well into the room before he saw that the prisoner on the floor held a rifle across his knees.

Mitch halted in midstride. For all his bulk, he had quick reflexes; surprise didn't slow him much. One startled look, and then the gun was lifting in his hand.

Johnny Logan shot him.

The heavy slug smashed him full in the chest. The man who had killed Bob Early was driven back a step, pivoted on one bootheel and went down, the gun falling from his hand and spinning across the floor to a stop a couple of yards from Johnny. Falling, Mitch revealed the other two who had entered just behind him — and showed them the smoking rifle pointed in their direction. They froze. Johnny Logan pinned his attention on Durkin and told the gunman, in a voice that did not sound like his own: "Lift your iron, and throw it out into the yard. I'll kill you if you don't!"

Through the swirl of stinking muzzle smoke, Durkin looked at the rifle and at the dead man lying at his feet. Gingerly, with exaggeratedly careful movements, he picked the revolver out of his holster, using thumb and two fingers. Turning, he flipped it out through the open door. He looked again at Johnny, his face holding a strange mix of baffled rage, surprise, fear — and a sudden new respect.

Johnny Logan ordered, "Both of you put your hands on top of your heads, and stand hitched till I say you can move." Two pairs of arms lifted in unison.

All at once Johnny was shaking, from reaction and from the effort all this had cost him. But the swift events of these last minutes had cleared his head, and he was alert and cautious as he reached up, got hold of the bunk frame and pulled himself to his feet. He braced himself, and waited while the room stopped pitching and settled. Afterwards he moved forward a step, went to one knee and rose again, holding the revolver Mitch had dropped. It was a handier weapon than the rifle, and he laid the latter on the bunk behind him. Looking at his prisoners, he gave his head a jerk to swing the black mane of hair back from his dark face.

The savage anger inside him must have shown. The baldheaded man, who had not spoken a word, suddenly found his voice. "Look!" he cried shakily. "I'm only the cook. I ain't part of this . . ."

"The hell you're not!" Johnny retorted. "So don't make any mistakes." He waggled his gunbarrel toward the fallen table. "Pick up the table, and see if you can get that broken leg propped. As for you," he added, switching his hawkish stare to Chet Durkin, "don't move a muscle!"

Neither man appeared to have any thought just then of defying the Indian. Durkin had looked a little green from the moment he saw Mitch drop at his feet. The cook hastened to do as he had been ordered, righting the table and worrying the leg back into position.

Suddenly Anne was in the doorway. She had picked up Durkin's revolver. She held it in both hands as she peered, wild-eyed and breathless, about the room. She looked askance at the body on the floor, and then she hurried to Johnny, who moved to one side so that she wouldn't come between him and his prisoners. From the expression on her face, he could judge that his own must look pretty bad after its contact with Mitch's bruising fists. "I'm all right," he gruffly answered her stammered query. "But, what are *you* doing here? I told you —"

"I know what you told me. But I *couldn't* let you ride on alone, not knowing what you might be getting into!"

**151**

"Lucky for me, at that," he conceded. "Do you know something about that rattler in the corral?"

"Of course. I saw you were in trouble, so I caught it and threw it in there. I hoped it would stir up the horses, maybe give me a chance to slip you your rifle . . ."

Johnny touched her cheek, and there was a feeling of wonder in him. "Where do they find girls like you?" he exclaimed.

He turned back to his prisoners. Durkin, taking him literally, still stood with his hands clasped atop his head, not moving. The table had been set up again. Johnny told Durkin, "All right. You sit down." And to the girl: "See if you can find me something to write with."

There was a shelf above the space heater that sat in a box of cinders near one wall of the bunkhouse. Anne rummaged through the odds and ends of magazines and paperbound books, and came back with a cheap tablet and a pencil stub. Johnny thanked her and jerked his head at Durkin. "They're for him."

She placed them on the table. Durkin scowled at the tablet and then at Johnny. "Just what am I supposed to do with this?"

"You'll write down everything your friend Mitch told me awhile ago."

"I will, like hell!"

"Think not?" Johnny's eyes turned to flint, and the bore of the gun in his hand rose to point directly at the man's face. "You'll write it all. About the Cherokee Strip, about poaching on the ranchers' beef and the

152

killing of Bob Early, and Brady's plan to take what he wants of the reservation." His mouth twisted. "I know perfectly well, nobody'd even listen if an Indian came in with a story like that. But a statement by one of Brady's gunmen — they'll at least have to pay attention!"

A moment longer Durkin tried to meet his look with defiance, but something in Johnny's face — and in the unblinking menace of the gun — must have changed his mind. With an ugly scowl he picked up the pencil, flipped through the tablet to a clean page and in a dead silence laboriously began to write.

Finished, he flung the pencil down and looked coldly at Johnny. The latter, not wanting to take his eyes off his prisoners, told the girl, "Read it to me, Anne."

She had some trouble following the half-literate scrawl, and once or twice she interrupted herself when she couldn't hold back an exclamation of astonishment and anger. "Johnny! Can this really be true?"

He nodded grimly. "All true, Anne. And it explains a lot." At his order, she tore out the tablet page, folded it and tucked it into the pocket of his shirt.

"It ain't gonna do you a damn bit of good," Durkin promised, sneering.

"We'll see. On your feet!"

"Why?" the gunman challenged. "What now?"

"You and I are taking a little ride," Johnny told him. "To see the sheriff . . ."

Under the muzzle of Johnny Logan's six-shooter, which he found in the brush were Durkin had thrown it, the gunman roped and saddled both horses from the

**153**

corral. Afterwards, with the cook's reluctant help, big Mitch's body was toted from the bunkhouse and tied, face down, across the saddle of the blue roan. Anne rode out of the timber, leading Johnny's black. While his prisoners sullenly waited, Johnny took the reins and then, standing beside the girl's mount, reached up to place a hand on her arm.

"You disobeyed me once," he said solemnly, "by not turning back when I told you — and it saved my life. But this time I mean it. I don't know what's going to happen when I get to town, but I can't have you to worry about. You've got to ride home — now!"

He could see the protest rising as her huge dark eyes searched his face, but then her expression relaxed, and her shoulders appeared to droop a little. She picked up the reins. "All right," she said in a small voice. She kicked her pony with a moccasined heel, and Johnny watched her ride away.

He knew she was hurt, but he couldn't have done anything else. It was frightening enough to think of the risks she had already run, by intervening here at B Cross. He shook his head and turned back, all business again, to find Chet Durkin watching him with an insolent smirk twisting his mouth. "You're really taking me to the sheriff?" he demanded loudly. "Don't you know you're wasting your time — and mine, too?"

Johnny merely looked at him; he could only hope he appeared surer of himself than he really felt. "Mount!" he ordered. With a shrug the prisoner obeyed, taking his time about it. Johnny toed the stirrup and swung astride his own black. A towrope anchored the roan, carrying Mitch's tarp-wrapped body, to his saddle horn. Johnny took up the reins in his left hand, leaving his right free for the gun that he had replaced in its holster. Looking down at the baldheaded cook, he said drily, "When Warren Brady shows up, I don't doubt, you'll be telling him everything that happened here. Just be sure you tell it straight!"

The man glowered at him sullenly. Johnny motioned Durkin out ahead and gave the black a kick. The extra horse and its swaying burden followed, as they took the well-defined set of wagon ruts marking the road to town.

The road lifted along the flank of a brushy hill just before it dropped into a saddle beyond, where the ranch would be lost to sight. A sudden tattoo of hoofbeats across the stillness made Johnny pull rein and twist sharply for a look back. He had a wide view of the ranch layout — and of the rider galloping northward away from the buildings, sunlight gilding the dust stirred up by the mount's pounding run. Johnny swore softly and started to reach for the rifle under his knee, but then he checked the movement.

He heard Durkin's malicious chuckle. "So Baldy didn't wait for the boss to show," the gunman said in high amusement. "He's off to find him and give the word of what's happened — and that gives *you* less time than you counted on. You never thought of that, I guess. Never even checked the barn, to see if there was another bronc he could use . . ."

Not bothering to answer, Johnny merely frowned. Swiftly calculating distances, he decided not to change his plan. He would just have to gamble that the cook couldn't warn Brady and Gannon in time for them to stop him reaching the sheriff's office with his prisoner. Right now, that was as far as he was trying to look.

Johnny drew a breath. Face expressionless, he told Chet Durkin, "Let's move along!"

It was clear that he could expect no help from Durkin. The prisoner stalled and did everything to hold them back; he pinned his hopes to the chance of being intercepted. Johnny swore at him, used his own rein ends to touch up the lagging brown horse and sting more speed out of it. At last he told the other man, in quiet fury, "If you want, I can bend this gun barrel over your skull and take you in across the saddle, like your friend Mitch. Is that what you're asking for? Or are you ready to settle down?"

Durkin turned sullen, but he no longer made trouble, and they were able to push ahead. As far as Johnny's nerves were concerned, however, the delay had done its work. He rode in a state of high tension, trying to watch the trail both behind and in front of them, not knowing where an attempt might be made to cut them off. But the miles fell back, and he could hardly credit it when he saw the roofs of town and realized they had actually made it without incident.

But that was not the end of it. Remembering the way he had left town the day before, he knew what he risked by showing himself again. His six-shooter was in his hand, its muzzle covering the prisoner riding slightly ahead, while his busy glance probed the side-walk canopies and every empty door and window as the town closed about them. He was surprised to see almost no life stirring anywhere along the twisting, dusty street. In puzzling contrast to the recent bustle and activity of Monroe's transient boomer population, there were no more than a half-dozen horses visible at the hitching posts, and nobody at all moving on the shaded walks. It looked more the way a cattle town might be expected to in the normal quiet of a week day afternoon.

But where were the boomers? They hadn't left. He could see their wagon camp, still occupying the flat beyond the town's edge. Johnny gave up the puzzle with a shrug. Whatever the explanation, he was grateful enough for the chance to slip in without, apparently, being noticed.

"Yonder," he told his prisoner curtly. "The jail office."

Durkin gave no answer as he jerked his animal's head in the direction indicated. Johnny followed him to the hitching rack, the roan trailing behind. As he was about to dismount, movement down the street suddenly caught his eye. He swung his head sharply. A familiar figure was crossing the empty street alone, picking his way over the dust and deep-etched ruts left by wagon wheels in boggy weather. He moved with an old man's stiff-jointed care, and Johnny saw a flash of white bandage beneath the low-crowned, wide-brimmed hat.

The old marshal seemed little the worse for being knocked down by the black horse during yesterday's escape. Johnny heaved a small sigh of relief.

He stepped down, anchored the black to the rail and drew a rifle from the saddle scabbard of the blue roan. He had holstered his six-shooter, and now he turned the rifle's muzzle on Durkin, who stood waiting and guardedly watching him. At that moment, from beyond the open door, Johnny heard angry voices.

He recognized them and hesitated in some dismay. He had hoped to find the sheriff alone. There being no option, Johnny grimly motioned Durkin ahead of him. The men inside appeared too engrossed in their quarrel to have noticed the horsemen arriving. Dallas Howbert was declaring with some heat, "Looks to me, Jenson, you've changed your tune some. Couple of days ago you were all for letting those Indians get away with any damn thing they felt like. I guess it makes a difference when it's *your* beef they take after!"

And Arne Jenson retorted, "I've said before, a steer or two hardly matters if those people are being cheated out of their rations. What changes everything is the murder of Bob Early!"

Then Johnny came through the door, herding his prisoner ahead of him. Sheriff Zach Gifford's ponderous bulk was sunk deep into his chair. Howbert sat across from him. Arne Jenson had been pacing, and he froze in mid-step, an arm raised, as all three stared at the newcomers. "The man who killed Bob Early," Johnny told them shortly, "is tied on the roan out front. But it was no Indian. He called himself Mitch, and he rode for Warren Brady."

"That's a lie!" Durkin cried hoarsely. "It's *all* lies!" He broke away from his captor and rushed forward, to appeal wild-eyed to the fat man behind the desk. "Thank God, I managed to stay alive until I got among white men again! Do something, sheriff! Shoot this red bastard — before he shoots me!" He really sounded like a man terrified for his life.

Johnny didn't even raise his voice. "Mitch confessed," he said coldly, "before I was forced to kill him. If you'll look at his bronc's hoofs, you'll see that the irons were deliberately pulled in order to lay a phony trail. And finally, there's this." He moved to the desk, elbowing Chet Durkin aside, and laid down the rifle he'd been holding. Silently he pointed to a dull glint of nailheads, driven into the stock to form letters that spelled out a name: "Bob."

Sheriff Gifford scowled at the rifle and then lifted his stare to Arne Jenson. "Early's?" he demanded.

The rancher nodded grimly and demanded of Johnny Logan, "Where did you find this?"

"In Brady's bunkhouse. Mitch didn't dare leave it behind. He knew any reservation Indian was bound to help himself to a weapon as good as this one, given the chance."

Durkin looked from one face to another and didn't like what he saw. He burst out in a new frenzy of indignation. "What the hell's going on here? You ain't *listening* to this lousy Injun? *I'm* telling you — a *white* man! — that everything he says is a lie!"

The sheriff regarded him without expression. "What's your name?"

"Chet Durkin. I ride for Brady, and I was right there and seen this red nigger gun Mitch Ewalt down without giving him a chance!" There was a froth of spittle at one corner of his mouth as he cried, "You wouldn't believe his word against a white man's, would you?"

No one answered, but Dallas Howbert suddenly pushed back his chair, the legs squealing on rough floorboards, rose abruptly and walked outside to where the horses were tied to the hitchrail. Through the window, the others could see him walk around the blue roan, raise a corner of the tarp and look at the face of the dead man. He leaned then and picked up a hoof to examine it.

Inside the office, Jenson was looking at Johnny Logan's face, swollen and battered by his beating at the fists of big Mitch. He said gruffly, "It appears you gave no mind to the advice I offered last night."

Johnny Logan couldn't keep resentment from showing. "I ain't obliged to follow orders from you, Mr. Jenson," he pointed out stiffly. "You fired me, and you let them turn you against the Cheyenne. That left me no choice but to try getting to the bottom of this thing on my own. It didn't look like there was anybody else who was even going to bother!"

What Jenson might have answered was lost as Dallas Howbert reentered, looking a little shaken. "No irons on the horse," he reported. "And the dead man — he was one of Brady's all right! I seen him in that bunch that came in here with Gannon. He's been shot in the chest, at close range. It ain't a pretty thing to look at!"

"Then we'll leave him right where he is for now," the sheriff decided firmly. The chair creaked under his ponderous weight; he turned his cold regard on Johnny

Logan. "Suppose you start at the beginning. Keep your story short, and make it true!"

Durkin broke in desperately. "You ain't actually going to listen to this —?"

"You'll have your turn," Gifford shut him off. "Go on, Logan. You'd better be convincing."

"I can show you the tracks of that roan horse," Johnny told him, "leading from the place where Bob Early was killed straight toward the reservation. I can show you where the killer tried to bury his trail and, when he thought he had, turned and headed for Brady's ranch instead. And where he threw away the meat from the steer he'd butchered."

"But how do you know," Howbert demanded, "that this Ewalt man you killed was the one riding the horse?"

"He admitted it — and the killing. He and this other fellow were fixing to kill me, and they'd have done it except I got a lucky break . . ."

"You hear?" cried Chet Durkin. "Is that story wild enough? Nobody in the world has imagination like a damn lyin' redskin!"

"All right," Arne Jenson challenged him. "If that was all lies, then let's hear your version."

"While he's at it," Johnny Logan suggested, taking a folded piece of paper from his pocket, "let him try to explain what he's written here."

As he offered the paper to Jenson, Chet Durkin made a lunge and grab for it. He almost got a hand on the paper, but Arne Jenson simply dealt him a backhanded blow that struck him in the chest and sent him staggering. A spur rowel caught in a crack of the floor, and Durkin was thrown off balance. He went down, and when he tried to scramble up again, he found himself looking into the muzzle of Jenson's gun.

"Just you take it easy," Jenson warned him, "while we see what we've got here."

Durkin looked at the gun. He touched his tongue to his lips, which seemed suddenly to have gone dry. He stayed on one knee, glowering blackly. Arne Jenson put away the gun and gave his attention to the writing on the paper.

The cattleman's eyes narrowed, his lips pursed in a soundless whistle, and he glanced at Johnny Logan — a look of pure astonishment. Then to Zach Gifford he said, "You better have a look at this!" The sheriff was a slow reader, and he silently mouthed the words to himself. When he had finished, he sat and stared at the paper for a long moment. Without comment, he simply handed it across the desk to Dallas Howbert.

All eyes turned to Chet Durkin, and their cold silence brought him stumbling to his feet, exclaiming harshly, "Hell! A man will do or say anything with a gun pointed at his head! The Indian told me what to write — he made up every word of it!"

"Out of whole cloth?" Jenson retorted. "I sort of doubt that! There's too much here that makes sense. It tells us, finally, just what Clayt Gannon is doing in this country. And it explains going after my beef and killing my rider, after they saw there was no other way to get me lined up against the Indians."

Dallas Howbert, through with the paper, laid it on the desk. He said heavily, "No man likes to admit he's been used for a fool. But who would ever have supposed Rawls and Brady were in this *together?*"

Jenson shrugged. "They fooled a whole range. But it begins to look like Nate Rawls may have got fooled the worst of anybody!"

Hearing such talk, seeing the looks on their faces, Johnny Logan began to feel the first stirrings of hope. If even Dallas Howbert had to recognize the truth, then perhaps there was a chance yet to break down part of the wall of prejudice against the Cheyenne. Just possibly, the cloud of doom hanging over the reservation showed the first faint signs of breaking . . .

Zach Gifford spoke, shaking his massive head at the document on the desk in front of him. "Regardless of how convincing *you* find this," he said heavily, "it ain't worth a damn."

Stung, Johnny Logan cried: "Every word of it's the truth!"

"I ain't talking about truth," the sheriff cut him off. "I'm talking legalities! Any judge would throw this kind of evidence out of court. All Durkin has to do is keep insisting you forced him to write it. That makes it one man's word against another's. And his skin is white. Yours ain't. It's as simple as that."

Chet Durkin appeared to swell visibly. His pockmarked cheeks rounded in a wide and triumphant grin. "What did I tell you?"

"The fact is, Logan," Zach Gifford continued, meeting Johnny's stunned look, "you've taken up my time to no purpose. There was no sound reason for bringing this man into my office."

"Are you saying I can go, sheriff?" Durkin asked.

A moment earlier he had been very close to panic. Now Gifford's curt nod seemed to lend him smug new confidence. He gave his trousers a hitch, and he actually seemed to enjoy the angry looks of Jenson and Howbert, which silently followed him to the door. There he turned, unable to resist a final thrust.

His words were heavy with menace, as his glance sought Johnny Logan. "Big Chief, you and me ain't finished. I'll be looking to settle for this. Don't think I won't!"

Johnny returned the stare bleakly. But he offered no answer, and the gunman turned to leave, his promise hanging in the stillness of the room.

# CHAPTER
# ELEVEN

Arne Jenson said sharply, "Hold it!"

With one foot on the threshold, Durkin turned. He stiffened under the rancher's stern eye. "You mean me?" he demanded belligerently.

Jenson simply crooked a beckoning finger. His other hand rested on the butt of his holstered gun, and Durkin was persuaded. Scowling fiercely, he came back into the room. There was reluctance in every move. Turning to the sheriff, Jenson said, "I been thinking. Even supposing that paper isn't any good in a courtroom, we can get some use from it!"

"I dunno how," Zach Gifford said gruffly.

"Haven't I heard you say, you wished you knew some way to get those boomers off your neck? This might do it. You told me they're holding a meeting of some kind this afternoon . . ."

The sheriff's puzzled scowl gave place to an expression of speculation. His eyes narrowed, all but lost in pouches of fat. "Maybe I follow you at that," he said slowly. And Johnny Logan, getting the drift of their meaning, exclaimed, "It might work. It just might."

"It can," Jenson told them, "if our friend here ain't loose to spoil the play, by shooting his mouth off at the wrong moment."

"All right." The lawman opened a drawer of the desk and took out a ring of keys. Pushing to his feet, he said, "A slight change of plans, Durkin."

"No!" Chet Durkin's whole body gave a jerk. "You ain't putting me in no cell!" As the sheriff came toward him, moving ponderously, Durkin backed away. Johnny thought he was on the verge of bolting, but the man checked himself when he saw Arne Jenson's gun slide once more from its holster. Durkin looked at the gun and then at the fat man. "You got no charge!" he cried hoarsely.

"I always can think of one," Gifford assured him and, with a shove of one meaty palm, sent his prisoner staggering toward the door to the jail corridor.

Durkin recovered and shouted. "Damn you! See how long I stay here, after Warren Brady finds out about this."

"Listen to me, you sonofabitch!" That was Arne Jenson, advancing on him, the gunbarrel lifting in his hand as though to strike. "Now that we've had the truth of this business out of you, I personally promise I'll make it stick somehow — if I have to bust your head to do it."

That seemed to break through the man's front of cocky brashness. His scarred cheeks lost color. Backing away from Jenson, he stumbled into the sheriff. To the latter he cried, "You gonna let him threaten me? You got to protect me, sheriff!"

166

"Then move!" the lawman snapped, and this time Chet Durkin let himself be hustled meekly enough along the corridor toward a waiting cell. Jenson called a pointed warning after him: "Think it over, mister. You might like it better in there — telling the law what it wants to hear — than outside where I can get my hands on you and *make* you talk!"

The loud metallic clang of the cell door broke the stillness of the jail office. Dallas Howbert, who had watched in silence, shook his head and said in a troubled tone, "It's just as well Brady *ain't* here. With one of his men jailed and another dead — that could complicate matters!"

"He may be here soon enough," Johnny Logan commented.

"What do you mean?"

"I forgot to tell you. Right after we left B Cross, we saw one of his men light out. It's pretty clear he went hunting for his boss and for Clayt Gannon."

The sheriff, returning from the cell, demanded, "What was that?" And Johnny repeated it. "The Clevenger place . . ."

Gifford scowled. "Ain't too much of a ride. It could depend on how they push their horses."

"Then we better move," Arne Jenson said. "Especially if we aim to catch that meeting before it breaks up."

Zach Gifford nodded and stepped to the desk, where he picked up Durkin's confession and pocketed it. "But I'll do the talking."

Johnny thought Jenson was going to argue about that, but the rancher let it pass. He looked at Dallas Howbert. "You coming with us?"

"Wouldn't miss it!" the other answered grimly.

The sheriff got his hat from its hook and, after a moment's hesitation, took down his gunbelt and holster and strapped them around his thick middle. He looked at Johnny, who had already started for the door. "Logan!" he ordered in a tone that made the Indian pause. "You'll stay here."

Johnny started to protest. The lawman cut him off. "I see no point deliberately riling those people. They may give us trouble, and again they may not — but if you're along, they're sure to! Besides, somebody has to be on hand, in case Brady shows before we're back. Keep him out of this jail and away from the prisoner. You understand?"

Disappointed as he was, Johnny Logan knew there was no argument against the sheriff's logic. He saw Arne Jenson's nod of agreement and shrugged. "You're the law . . ."

"One other thing," Dallas Howbert said suddenly. He was looking at Johnny, plainly ill at ease but with something he wanted to say. He got it out in a gruff burst: "Saturday — when we had our trouble, Logan — I didn't know about affairs on the reservation. I suppose it might have made a difference . . ."

Given with such poor grace, it was the nearest thing to an apology the man was capable of. Johnny settled for what he could get. "I didn't know then, either," he said.

**168**

And the three were gone. Alone, Johnny moved into the doorway and watched them cross the rutted street in the direction of the wagon camp.

The meeting seemed to be over, but luckily the men had not yet dispersed. They had separated into a number of small groups, standing amongst the weeds and trash and talking in loud and heated voices. Some of them stared in curious hostility as the three from the sheriff's office worked their way through the crowd.

"Judge" Rawls was seated on a wagon tongue, drinking from a tin cup that perhaps held coffee, perhaps something else. He had been laughing, but when he caught sight of the intruders, his expression changed. A wariness came into his eyes as he lowered the cup, revealing a swollen lip that made his mouth appear slightly lopsided — a memento, Arne Jenson supposed, of his fight with Johnny Logan yesterday in the newspaper office. Rawls tilted his head slightly to peer up at the newcomers, but the brim of the planter's hat he favored shaded the man's eyes and made them difficult to read.

"We heard you were holding a meeting," Zach Gifford said. He looked about him. "Or is it a council of war?"

"A little of both, maybe," Rawls countered. He upended his cup, tossed a few last drops to the dusty ground and set the cup on the wagon tongue beside him. "Something we can do for you, Gifford?"

A silence had begun, and it spread out like ripples on a pool. There was only the sound of men drawing the

**169**

circle narrower, keenly interested to learn what was afoot.

It was a warm day. Perspiring after his walk through the weeds and dust beyond the town limit, the sheriff pulled out a handkerchief and used it on his face and neck. He drew a breath before plunging in. "I got news," he began.

"So do we!" a voice broke in. "Go ahead, 'Judge'! Show 'em the telegram!" Rawls hesitated, obviously reluctant, but the boomer went right ahead. "The word from Washington is that a move's been started to drum up sympathy in Congress for opening the reservation. And here you been telling us, it would never happen!"

Arne Jenson demanded crisply, "Have you people any idea at all how long it could take, for a thing like that to be acted on? Are you planning to sit here all winter?"

"The hell with you, Jenson!" That was the red-bearded one, Stamper. His swollen, shapeless nose was another reminder of the sting of Johnny Logan's fists, and Jenson couldn't repress a kind of mean pleasure at seeing it. "We know how you sneer at the likes of us!" Stamper shouted angrily. "Men like you and Warren Brady — you've already grabbed off the land you need! But we got our rights, too, and nothing you can do will stop us claiming them!"

There was a dangerous murmur of agreement in the crowd, and for just a moment Arne Jenson felt acutely aware how heavily they outnumbered him and his companions. But Nate Rawls lifted a hand, and his voice imposed an uneasy quiet. "Come now!" Rawls

**170**

exclaimed. "There's been enough bad feelings. Let's find out just why these men are here."

Jenson shot the sheriff a look that warned him: *Make it strong!* The fat man cleared his throat. "Someone mentioned Brady," he began. "It happens we've turned up some evidence on him that we thought you people ought to know about. It concerns every one of you."

"Evidence?" "Judge" Rawls echoed in a tone of sharp suspicion.

"We been lied to," the sheriff went on, ignoring Rawls and speaking directly to the silent boomers. "Here's the proof of it." He brought Durkin's statement out of his pocket, unfolded it and held it up for all to see. "Here's a written confession, in his own hand, by one of Warren Brady's men — one of those professional gun-handlers he added to his crew a few weeks ago. This man's name is Durkin, and he's sitting in the jail right now, waiting for the law to settle with him. I want to read you what he has to say."

Suddenly Rawls was on his feet. "Let me look at that!"

"No!"

Gifford snatched the paper out of reach, and Rawls fumed. "You can't force your way into a private meeting!" he began.

Arne Jenson cut him off. "What's the matter, Rawls? You figure you might not *want* them to hear this? Or maybe," he added dryly, "you want first crack, to publish it in that newspaper of yours . . ."

Rawls glowered at him, feeling the point of Jenson's taunt. Jenson thought there was a faint shine of sweat on Rawls's sunken cheeks, an indication of just how perturbed he actually was. Stamper spoke. "Hell! Now you got our curiosity up, we better hear what this is all about." There was a clamor of agreement. Seeing the thing had gone too far to stop, Rawls subsided.

The sheriff cleared his throat and began to read. His voice was unnaturally tense.

When he had finished, there was silence for a moment. A gust of wind scattered dust and campfire ash and struck the canvas of a wagontop with a report like a pistol shot. Stamper turned to Rawls and demanded, "Well? What do *you* say?"

Rawls looked stunned. His cheeks had lost color, and when he tried to speak, his voice came out in a croak. "Lies!" he cried hoarsely, as Durkin had before him, and then louder: "All *lies!*"

"You've been lying from the start, haven't you?" Arne Jenson challenged. "Both you and Brady — pretending you're enemies, that you aren't together in this scheme to steal the Cheyennes' land. After deceiving these followers of yours, it'd be no more than you deserve to have Brady grab off the lion's share and leave you with nothing at all!"

Rawls shook his head, trying to voice a denial. He was plainly in a state of shock, and for once speech failed him. Nothing more than incoherent sounds came out. He wasn't able to defend himself when big Stamper suddenly grabbed him by the front of his coat. "Look at me, damn you!" Rawls's wide-brimmed hat was dislodged as the red-bearded man hauled him around. Rawls blinked near-sightedly into the sunlight that struck his unshielded face.

"You and Brady *did* have some kind of a deal! That's the truth, ain't it?" the boomer shouted. "And you know now, it's the truth, he means to double-cross the lot of us with that tough crew he hired — just like the sheriff says!"

"I had a cousin made that Cherokee Strip run," somebody else spoke up when Rawls seemed unable to answer. "He told me afterwards, it was plain murder! My cousin managed to hold onto his claim, because it wasn't worth nothing to begin with. But the nightriders had all the good ones spotted, and on every side of him men got cleaned off their holdings, and beaten up or killed if they tried to fight back. I never bargained on getting into anything like *that!* Or putting my family through it . . ."

Someone else said loudly, "We have a right to protection! What the hell have we got a sheriff for?"

"With one deputy?" Zach Gifford retorted. "Sorry, but my office ain't set up to handle a job that size, even if I felt obliged to."

"The army, then?" That brought nothing but scornful stares. The man looked around wildly. "Well, damn it," he cried, "I guess we can fight for our own! There's more of us than any tough crew Brady could have hired."

"And while I'm busy helping you hold *your* claim," Stamper reminded him, "they come around and grab mine behind my back! No, a situation like that, it's everybody for himself — and everybody loses!"

Suddenly he had hold of "Judge" Rawls again and was shaking him. "That's what *you* done to us. It's what we get for listening to your talk!"

There was a ripping of cloth. Rawls broke free and stumbled backward, part of his coatfront torn and hanging loose. He swung his head and peered about blindly. Then, like a man in a daze, he turned without a word and started away at a loose and shambling gait.

Howbert made a move as though to stop him. Jenson shook his head. "Let him go! Nate Rawls has just had the shock of his life. It'll do him good to go sit in that newspaper office and brood about it awhile . . ."

Zach Gifford refolded the paper and returned it to his pocket. "Well, there you have it," the sheriff said bluntly. "If I were you men, I'd start doing some hard thinking."

"Think about *this*." Arne Jenson lifted his voice above the rising murmur of angry talk. "For all his bragging, Rawls ain't the only one that knows people in Washington. If I have to go back there myself, I aim to see some attention gets paid to the Cheyenne and what's been done to them. Take my word for it, you're all backing a game you can't win. Get out of it — now! You've put yourselves and your families through enough hardship, for nothing."

"Amen to that!" Dallas Howbert added roughly.

Looking around, Jenson could see nothing but angry bitterness and sullen resentment, and his mouth set hard. "Very well." He turned to his companions. "We've said all we can. It's up to them now."

Deliberately he turned his back on that scowling and disappointed group. Howbert and the sheriff walked away after him. Silence lay heavy in their wake.

Chet Durkin was worked up and unable to stop talking. From his cell he shouted at Johnny Logan, abuse and filth mingling with promises of dire revenge. "You damned red-skinned sonofabitch! You ain't keeping me in here, not after Brady and Clayt Gannon show up. They'll have me loose, and when they do —" Johnny paused in his pacing of the office, pivoted on one heel, seized the cellblock door and slammed it shut, cutting off the prisoner's rasping voice.

After that it was possible to think.

His uneasiness had grown as time dragged, and he waited alone in the jail office. He didn't really think there was much danger of trouble at the boomer camp — probably far less, he had to admit, than if he had insisted on going along with Jenson and the sheriff. But Johnny had a feeling, a premonition, that this matter wasn't going to end without violence. After all, carefully laid plans had been exploded. And as Chet Durkin promised, Warren Brady would see to it that someone paid.

On his own initiative Johnny had led the horses — his black and the roan with Mitch's stiffening body still lashed to it — around behind the jail and tied them there, out of the way. He saw no sense in calling needless attention to them. Now he dropped into Gifford's swivel chair and sat staring moodily at the door, listening to any sound outside and wondering how the business at the boomer camp was going.

When he heard voices and a clomping of boots along the sidewalk, he thought it might be Jenson and the others returning. He leapt quickly to his feet. When he reached the door, the voices had passed by and faded again. Impatiently Johnny flung open the door and stepped outside. A pair of cowpunchers disappeared into a saloon a few doors on, leaving the batwings stirring behind them and the expanse of dust and weather-beaten buildings as silent as before.

The slot between a couple of buildings opposite framed a narrow view of the wagon camp — a mere glimpse of dirt-streaked canvas and a yellow pall of dust and smoke that always seemed to hang motionless there, despite the steady wind. Leaning his shoulder against the doorframe, Johnny Logan stared long and thoughtfully at that dust stain. He was half-listening for something to break the somnolent stillness. A gunshot, maybe?

And then he did hear a sound, and it instantly straightened him, every sense alert. Up at the end of the street, a clot of horsemen had just entered town and were coming on toward the jail at a steady pace. In some way the sight held a hint of grim and dangerous purpose.

The breath clogged in his throat as he turned back into the office, hastily searching. He had his six-shooter, but he needed more reach, and he had forgotten to take his own saddle gun out of its scabbard. Then he saw Bob Early's rifle lying on the

**176**

desk and stepped over for it. His palm smoothed the well-worn stock embossed with brass nailheads. He worked the lever, jacking a shell into the breach, as he moved back to the door. Taking up a post slightly back from the opening, he watched Warren Brady approach with Clayt Gannon beside him and two other men close behind. All four were armed with belt guns and carried rifles on their saddles.

Someone else had seen or heard them: Johnny's prisoner let out a yell: "Clayt!" His voice sounded thinly in the quiet street. Johnny could picture him clinging to the window bars, craning to peer along the jail's side wall. "Clayt! Can you hear me?"

Johnny saw the riders pull to a halt. Clayt Gannon looked about him, "Durkin?"

"I'm back here! In a cell! Get me out, damn it!" the prisoner exclaimed, as heads turned and finally located him. "You got nobody to stop you," Durkin promised. "Just that Injun. Sheriff left him to hold down the jail by himself."

Out in the street, Gannon and Warren Brady exchanged a look. Gannon demanded, "Why the hell would the sheriff do that?"

"Never mind!" the prisoner retorted. "Just get me out of here. The four of you can take him."

Johnny Logan's hands had a tight grip on the rifle. Through the open door he called out sharply. "I wouldn't try it."

That had an effect. Though he had been careful to stay back from the opening, the room shadows might have held some glint of the rifle's barrel. At any rate, no

**177**

one reached for a gun or made any move to approach, but the two men behind Brady and his foreman quickly spread out to offer a poorer target. Johnny could not keep them all in his sights at once.

He aimed the muzzle at Warren Brady and held it steady, while an eddy of warm wind raked the street and scattered hoof-raised dust. The dust devil bothered the horses, stinging their hides, and they had to be settled with some cursing and jerking of the reins.

There was still no other stir of life in the empty street — no indication that the town sensed that anything unusual was happening.

Brady conferred with his foreman and received some curt answer. The rancher raised his voice then, and it was crisp with anger. "Logan, if that's what they call you! You came to my place today, killed one of my men and took another at gun point. Now are you going to step out here, where I can talk to you?"

"I'll stay where I am," Johnny Logan called back. "You can do your talking with the sheriff."

Brady chewed on that a moment. He appeared to decide against arguing the point, because his next words were for the man in the cell. "Durkin, I'm told you wrote something . . ."

"I had to," Durkin said. "The Injun was holding a gun at my head."

"Do you know what became of it?"

"The sheriff has the paper — him and Jenson and another. They took it to show that crowd at the boomer camp. They been gone nearly half an hour."

Brady swore. Johnny could see the flash of his eyeglasses as his head jerked under the impact of this news. And Johnny couldn't resist ramming the point home. "You see what it means, Brady? You set out to use everybody — the Cheyenne, the boomers, the other cattlemen — even 'Judge' Rawls, your partner in the scheme to steal the reservation. But now the truth is out, you've lost your chance to make it work!"

The rancher's head swung back; understanding was written in his face. "And who have I got to thank for this?" Warren Brady cried in bitter rage. "One lousy Indian?"

"One Indian, that's right!" Johnny shot back. "Do you want to turn your white-eye gunslingers loose on me? Now's your chance!" Reckless impulse carried him out through the doorway, into full view, with the stock of Bob Early's weapon braced against his hip. He said, "This rifle belonged to a man your toughs murdered. It's aimed right at your heart, Brady!"

There was moisture on his palms, and sweat trickled down his ribs. But anger was high in Johnny Logan just then, and it swamped any trace of caution. His finger, tight on the trigger of the rifle, started to take up the slack. He waited for his enemies to make the next move.

Then a voice was shouting Warren Brady's name hoarsely. Across the way, a man came at a stumbling run into the street, directly under the nose of the rancher's mount. It was "Judge" Rawls. His clothing was torn and disheveled. He had lost his planter's hat, and rumpled hair stood wild on his head. He looked as though he had run all the way from the boomer camp, perhaps had run for his very life.

"Damn you, Brady!" he shouted. His eyes had an almost insane glint in them. "I want to know, is there truth to that paper the sheriff's showing around? Have you been planning all along to use your guns against my people and throw them off their claims?"

Warren Brady looked down at the man, trying to read the state of his emotions and debating if there was any point in further pretense. Apparently he decided things had gone too far. It was in a tone suggesting cold boredom that he said, "Of course it's true!"

"You've *ruined* me!" Rawls was nearly screaming. His politician's voice, trained for oratory, carried loudly. "Do you understand? No one will ever again believe a word I tell them! You can't use me like that and —"

He reached for Brady, trying to haul him from the saddle. The rancher shook him off and, with a look of contempt, swung a booted foot. The heavy stirrup smashed Rawls full in the chest and sent him staggering, both hands clutching at the pain that filled his chest.

Without expression, Warren Brady yanked the gun from his holster and fired point-blank.

The horses snorted and shied. The revolver shot slapped echoes off building fronts along the street. "Judge" Rawls, thrown backward, stumbled on the edge of the rough boardwalk and fell hard against a lathe-turned wooden post holding up a storefront arcade. Still clutching his middle, he crumpled slowly.

**180**

He slid down the post and brought up at the foot of it, still peering wide-eyed at Warren Brady through a melting haze of powdersmoke.

# CHAPTER
# TWELVE

Warren Brady checkreined the nervous animal under him and blandly eyed the man he had shot. Johnny Logan was stunned by the unexpectedness of it. Then doors opened and windows ran up, voices shouting questions as the town came alive to the sound of gunfire at the jail.

Still holding the smoking gun, Warren Brady stepped down from his sorrel and dropped reins to anchor it. He walked over to look at the man he had shot. "Judge" Rawls was breathing shallowly through slack lips. His eyes were glazed, and his sweat-beaded face turned pale and bloated as the cheek muscles loosened in bullet shock. Blood was seeping between the fingers clasped tight over the wound in his belly. Brady did not touch the hurt man; there was no trace of compassion in him as he shoved the weapon back into its holster.

Boots struck the boardwalk. Brady lifted his head to face Arne Jenson and Dallas Howbert, who had just followed Nathan Rawls out of the weed-grown path leading from the boomer encampment. They stared at him across the crumpled shape of his victim. It was Howbert who exclaimed, "By God, we saw what happened! We saw you deliberately put a bullet in him!"

"Did Rawls make a scene?" Jenson demanded harshly. "Because he'd learned how he'd been used? Is that why you shot him?"

The other returned a look that was cold as ice and answered curtly, "He was trying to get at the Derringer he carries in his waistcoat pocket. I had to shoot him — in self-defense."

Johnny Logan, watching from the jail doorway, almost spoke up to protest that the judge hadn't been reaching for any weapon — he had simply reeled back from the drive of Brady's kick, clutching his chest, where the heavy stirrup struck. But then Johnny hesitated, Brady *could* have thought Rawls was reaching for a gun.

Johnny hesitated, doubtful. "Judge" Rawls toppled sideways and rolled onto his face. His body lay half in the street dust and half in the shadow of the gallery. Arne Jenson shoved Howbert aside and dropped to one knee, taking the wounded man by a shoulder. Jenson turned him face upward, but the limpness of the body showed clearly enough that the man was finished. The dead hands, dropping away, revealed the bloody damage the bullet had done. Gingerly Arne Jenson checked the waistcoat pockets. His head lifted then, and he looked directly at Brady.

"There's no gun," he said bleakly. "Whatever you may have *thought* you were doing, you've killed an unarmed man!"

The words hung in the stillness. But if Warren Brady was appalled at his mistake, he gave no sign of it. Johnny Logan thought the man shrugged indifferently,

**183**

as Jenson straightened to his feet. Sheriff Gifford hurried belatedly on the scene. The lawman's bulk was against him, and he wheezed from the effort, sweat streaming down the gross cheeks of his red face. He looked at the gaunt shape of the dead man and demanded harshly, "Who done this? Who fired the shot?"

"He did!" Dallas Howbert seized Gifford by an arm and tried to propel him toward Warren Brady, who stood defiantly in the center of the street, his armed riders ranged behind him. For all his lack of size and unimpressive features, he was a dangerous figure as he faced his accusers. "Jenson and me both seen it!" Howbert declared loudly. "It was plain murder! Nate Rawls maybe wasn't too much of a man, but he deserved a better death than that! I demand that Brady be put under arrest!"

You could see Gifford's painful indecision. His world had been turned upside down. Plainly, he had never thought to put the weight of the law on anyone he respected as much as he had always respected the owner of the B Cross. But the sheriff was no coward. With an angry gesture he shook off Howbert's grasp, and a breath swelled his heavy frame as he took a single, meaningful step toward Warren Brady.

A signal seemed to pass between Clayt Gannon and Brady's other two riders. They stiffened in their saddles, and Gannon's lean hand made a move to sweep back the skirt of his denim jacket, clearing the weapon in his holster. Arne Jenson saw. "No hired guns, Gannon!" he exclaimed, as he started to bring

184

out his own revolver. As though acknowledging Arne Jenson as the real leader here, Clayt Gannon drew and fired with a single smooth motion. Jenson was picked up, spun about and slammed hard into the dirt.

Johnny Logan heard himself shouting. Until that instant he had stood rooted; it was sight of Arne Jenson going down that jarred him loose. Only as he lunged forward, and Gannon's head swung toward him, did he remember that Bob Early's rifle hung forgotten in his hand. It seemed to weigh a ton as he fought to bring it up. He caught the barrel in his left hand and worked the trigger just as Gannon's revolver exploded almost in his face.

Gannon's horse reared above Johnny. The horse pawed in terror at the double smash of shots. The steel shoes came down, missing Johnny by inches. The hoofs slammed the ground so hard, he felt the ground shake. Then a choking swirl of dust and powdersmoke parted, and he saw the empty saddle. Clayt Gannon was lying face down in the street, his six-shooter smoking beneath one limp, out-flung hand.

Slowly Johnny lowered the rifle, his own hands shaking with the realization he was unharmed. His lungs swelled on a tremulous breath tanged with powder stink. He lifted his head.

The whole street was aboil with the excitement of yelling men, who came running from every direction. But here at its center, things were oddly still, as those remaining on their feet stared at the figures sprawled motionless in the dust. In their midst a frail old man, with a bandage under his hat and a town marshal's

**185**

badge pinned to his rusty black frock coat, had appeared from somewhere. He gripped a hog-leg revolver with both hands to hold it steady on the pair of mounted gunmen who sat stunned by what had happened to Clayt Gannon.

"You roosters better stay put," he warned them, in an ancient voice that still crackled with danger. "Both of you! The town's had its quota of gunsmoke for one afternoon. It ends right here and now . . ."

Arne Jenson asked, in a voice shaken by pain, "Where's Warren Brady?"

"They got him in jail," Johnny said shortly. "In the same cell with Chet Durkin — a fitting place for him." Gannon and Mitch and "Judge" Rawls were on tables in the back room at the undertaker's, he might have added. At the boomer camp, men were already loading their gear and their families back in the wagons that had brought them to this country. It had been a day of dramatic changes and reversals.

Logan and Jenson were too exhausted to do much talking — Jenson from the ordeal of having a .45 slug dug out of his shoulder, Johnny from helping hold him on the operating table while a whiskered frontier surgeon did his work. Thoroughly spent, Johnny sat by the cot in the doctor's sick room, dusty hat on his knees. His former boss looked as white as the pillow or the bulky bandage. Jenson had drained off half the glass of whiskey on the table beside him; that appeared to restore some of the strength the wound had taken from him.

**186**

"How are you feeling?" Johnny asked anxiously.

"I ain't staying *here* long!" the rancher promised. "I got telegrams to send. And if they don't do the job, then I can't waste any time heading for Washington City. Those shenanigans at the reservation have got to be stopped!"

Johnny frowned. "The doctor says, with that arm —"

"Hell with the doc! It's my arm, ain't it?" Jenson shifted position angrily. He saw his smoke-blackened pipe lying on the table and tried to reach for it with his good hand. Johnny quickly got the pipe and the sack of rough cut, and began to fill the bowl for him.

The hurt man watched, frowning as though there were something he did not quite know how to phrase. Finally he demanded, "Where will you be going from here?"

"The reservation," Johnny answered, attention on what his hands were doing. "Someone I know is going to be mighty anxious to hear what happened."

He had never mentioned Anne, though he thought the other probably suspected he had a girl. But Jenson had something else in mind. "I mean, afterwards," he said, with an impatient shake of his head. "You're coming back to work for me, ain't you?"

"Johnny's brown hands went still. "You fired me . . ."

"Hell, I know that! You're sore at me for it — and especially for letting myself be duped into blaming the Cheyenne for poor Bob Early's killing. I won't try to justify that by sayin' I had to believe the evidence. I'd just be pleased if you could overlook it, and come back to work as if nothing happened."

Taking his time, Johnny covered his reluctance to answer by handing the man his charged pipe and, still not meeting his eyes, thumbing a match for Jenson to suck flame into the bowl. He could feel the other's frown probing his face, through the spurting wreath of blue-grey smoke. He shook out the match and dropped it on the floor beside his boots.

"It couldn't be the same," he said heavily. "You same as told me I was let go to keep the crew from taking it out on me, because of what happened to Bob. Do you think, knowing that, I could go back to sharing a bunkhouse with them? When I used to hope they had at least come to tolerate me . . ."

Arne Jenson tried to protest. "That ain't fair! We all been upset — and men will do and say things they wouldn't ordinarily. Give us another chance, boy!"

Johnny raised his head and looked directly at the man. "I guess you really mean that." But words he had recently spoken to Anne were strong in his mind, and he shook his head. "No hard feelings. It's just that I been thinking for some time, I ought to leave this place. Maybe now I've had a sign that this is the right moment for me to go."

"Go where?" Jenson demanded roughly.

He could only shake his head. "I don't know, Mr. Jenson. I really don't. A fellow like me — both Indian and white, yet not really either one — what have I got a right to look for? I only know I haven't found it here." Restlessly he surged to his feet, and stood hat-in-hand looking down at the man in the bed. "Maybe it ain't to be found anywhere. But I got to look! Can you see that?"

A long stare held, and then the older man sighed and wagged his head against the pillow. "I reckon nobody else could really know what it's like inside that head of yours, Johnny. So go ahead! Do what you have to! If you never find what you're looking for — well, you savvy that the trail you follow away from here leads back again. You'll always be welcome at Bar J. Anytime!"

"Thanks, Mr. Jenson. For more than I can tell you." Impulsively Johnny stuck out his hand, and the white man took it.

Moments later, Johnny Logan let himself out the side door and walked down the path to the front of the house, where the doctor's shingle, swinging from the porch overhang, creaked faintly in a strengthening wind. The house sat on a slight rise, with a view dominating the town below. The arching sky would soon darken, lights already glowed in the town, and yonder at the wagon camp a few fires burned. Woodsmoke lay like a dark shelf above the haphazard scattering of people and animals and belongings.

Perhaps he imagined it, but the camp looked different. There was something subdued about it now. The beaten aura of land-hungry men who had lived on a shoddy dream and seen it fade. Now they couldn't wait to leave. Even as Johnny watched, a couple of wagons pulled out, yells sounding faintly as the drivers whipped their teams and pointed them wherever the road might lead through the coming night. In a few

**189**

days more, the last of them would be gone without a trace.

For just a moment Johnny felt a tinge of pity, but at once his bronzed and hawkish face grew hard again. These had been merely the losers — the inefficient — in the scramble to grab off land that until yesterday had been the Indian's ancient heritage. You could pity their women and their children, maybe, but there was nothing pathetic about the white man's greed. That was simply ugly.

Johnny Logan breathed deeply of the night odors, walked out to his waiting horse and lifted into the saddle.

| APL | | CCS | |
|-----|---|-----|---|
| Cen | | Ear | |
| Mcb | | Cou | |
| ALL | | Jub | |
| WH | | CHE | |
| Ald | | Bel | |
| Fin | | Fol | |
| Can | | STO | |
| Til | | HCL | |